HIS BEAUTY

JACK HARBON

For Adrian, solely because you hate how often I write Beauty and the Beast retellings. Ah, you mad.

CONTENT WARNING

Graphic violence, on-page sex, interspecies sex, murder, kidnapping, animal death, familial death, gendered slurs, and threats of sexual violence.

HIS BEAUTY

"**H**e's been gone too long, Isla," Elyse says, bursting into my room with a cloud of anxiety following behind her. She wrings her thin hands together, brown eyes wide with worry. She's the spitting image of our mother, down to her golden hair and cherubic face, and it brings me back to when I was a girl, and Mother would pace back and forth, impatiently waiting for our father to return home.

"I'm sure he's fine," I say calmly, reaching for her. She's only a few years younger than me, but my maternal instinct can't help but kick in when she's around. "He's okay. It's just taking longer than usual, that's all."

"Isla, he left four hours ago. It was supposed to be easy. It's taking too long. He's in danger."

I resist the urge to sigh at her dramatic nature. It would only further upset her, and right now, I just need her to calm down. "Where did he go, anyway? I thought he was just going into town to get food."

It's not unusual for our father to spend time in the village a few miles east. Pickpocketing has been a talent of his since before we were born. He's nimble and unsuspecting, and because of this, he's managed to give us a somewhat decent life. Not one of luxury, not by any means, but we're not any closer to poverty. Humble. That's the word he's always used to explain our situation.

The two-bedroom cottage doesn't have a plumbing system indoors, but we have a roof over our heads and food on the table every night. *Mostly* every night. We're safe here, and it's because of him. Mother would always stress herself into a head of gray hair, thinking about all the trouble he could face were he caught by authorities. East Graybrook doesn't take kindly to thieves, and the punishment is often cruel.

Father's always managed to provide for us, and to this day, he hasn't been caught.

"He wasn't going into town," Elyse says in a shrill voice. "He was going to Highburn."

My heart sinks to my feet, and I feel my throat grow tight. "No," I say, shaking my head. No, he wouldn't go somewhere that dangerous. He wouldn't risk his life stepping foot on that property. Our father might be reckless, but he's not a fool. This has to be a misunderstanding.

"He told me he was headed to Highburn Hold. This was supposed to be his last trip. He wanted to make sure we had enough when he...when he..." Elyse chokes up, and her eyes well with tears. She can't even bring herself to say the words.

"When he dies," I whisper.

It's not far off. He's gotten progressively sicker. Most days, he barely has an appetite. His stomach is killing him; that's what the physician in East Graybrook told us when we visited two years ago. Ever since then, he's lost weight, his body growing more and more frail as the days pass. Soon, he'll shut down entirely, and after that, he'll be reunited with our mother. I feel the sting of tears prickle my eyes too, but I tilt my head back and sniff hard.

"He's a damn fool," I whisper, shaking my head. "He's going to get himself killed."

"I shouldn't have let him go," Elyse cries. She buries her face in her hands and sobs. "I should have stopped him. I should've gone this time."

"No, Elyse," I say, grabbing her shoulders. "You went last time. It was his turn."

"He's dead. I know he is. I can feel it, Isla. Father

was caught by that...that monster. And he's killed him."

I can't believe that. I refuse to believe it. "I'm going to get him back," I say. Her head snaps up, and she looks at me like I've lost my mind.

"Isla, no! You can't."

"What am I supposed to do? Leave him out there? What if he just got hurt or something? What if he needs my help?"

She opens her mouth like she wants to argue but closes it, swiping at her tears. "Go find him," she says, her eyes hardening. "Go find him and bring him home. Please."

I pull my sister into my arms for a tight hug. "I'll be back soon. With Father."

When I pull away, my heart squeezes tight. I can't let her down. I have to bring him back, or at the very least, find out what's taking him so long to return. I change into a pair of trousers, boots, and a red cloak and head out to the back of the cottage. There, I open the door to Isabelle's stable. She lifts her head up at the noise, shuffling in place. It's as if she knows there's something wrong. Like she can sense my urgency.

"Belle," I say, running my hand along her neck. "It's time to go, sweetheart." Carefully, I lead her out of the stable and toward the road. Elyse stands by the front door, a shawl wrapped around her body and puffs of air escaping her lips in small clouds. I give her a short nod and mount Isabelle, taking hold of the reins and leading her onto the dirt path.

"Wait up for me," I tell Elyse.

"Always."

With a quick gesture, I lead Isabelle down the path, urging her to move faster. The possibilities of my father's fate race through my mind, and I fight hard to block them out. He's fine. Then I remember where he is. Highburn Hold.

It's a cursed castle. I've heard stories of the monster that lives within its walls. They say he's indescribable, a beast full of bloodlust, and a hunger for the souls of the innocent. A nightmare come to life, always on the verge of destroying Graybrook. He's been whispered about for as long as I can remember, and if even half of what the townspeople say is true, Father is in more danger than ever before.

As we race through the woods, the bitter wind whips at my face and sends my brown hair flying in every direction. I snap my head and clear my vision, squinting as Isabelle darts around a bend and bounds over a fallen tree. She takes me through the harsh river with only a few issues, but when we return to solid ground once more, she's lightning.

It takes nearly a half-hour to arrive outside of

Highburn Hold, and when we do, I pull back on the reins and stare up at the towering building. It's as beautiful as it is terrifying, with snowcapped spires shooting toward the sky and weathered stone walls surrounding it. Movement down below catches my attention, and I see Father's horse, Gwen, sniffing around.

"Oh, no..."

I hop from Isabelle's back and carefully ease my way down the shallow cliff toward Gwen. Leading around the wall is a set of footprints that I can only assume to be Father's. "Hi, darling," I whisper to the steed, running my fingers through her mane as I gather my courage. "He went this way, didn't he?"

Gwen gives me a lazy blink and huffs out an answer I can't understand. There's no turning back. If Father is here, I have to save him. I adjust the cloak on my shoulders and begin following the footprints. They go on for ages until finally, they stop at a crack in the base of the building. It's as if the weight of the building has shifted, causing the stones to crumble. It's barely big enough for a person to fit through, and I slip through the hole, grateful to be shielded from the harsh wind.

At least I am in the beginning. When my eyes adjust, and I can see more, I gasp. It's a dungeon. I'd heard tales of prisoners in Highburn, but I assumed they were just that. There was no way a man could be wicked enough to have something like that in his home. But as I step deeper into the cavernous room, I can clearly make out the three cages lining the far right wall. They're all empty. All but the last one.

A figure hunches over in a pile of fabric, a small pool of blood snaking off along the stone. I approach tentatively, whispering. "Father?"

I recognize the groan the person lets out. I've heard it many times before; when my father's stomach pains grew too much to bear. When we forced him to eat, even though he felt no need to. He rolls onto his side and looks up at me. His face is bloodied like he's been beaten.

"Father!" I cry, tears springing to my eyes. "What —what happened to you? Who did this?" I tug on the bars, foolishly hoping that I have enough strength to pry him free. All it does is chill my hands painfully. "I have to get you out," I say, searching for something, *anything* that I can use to free him. There has to be a way to break him out.

"Isla?" Father pushes himself from the cement slowly, crawling to the metal bars that imprison him. "What are you doing here? You shouldn't have come."

"I couldn't leave you! I came to bring you home. You should've never come here." I can't help the anger in my voice. He's smarter than this. He had to have known the risk of doing something this reckless.

"I needed to protect you and your sister. Provide...when I'm gone." There's anguish in his voice, and he shamefully drops his gaze. I fall to my knees before him, holding his hands through the bars.

"You can't think like that. There's still plenty of time before that happens, Papa." When I use that name, the one I stopped using when I was a girl, his gaze rises to mine, and his eyebrows knit together sadly.

"My Isla... I love you. But you have to go. He's going to come back, and I'd die before I let him hurt you."

"Who?"

"The Beast of Highburn. The stories are true. They're *true*."

"All of them?"

He must be mistaken. The horrors I've heard... The carnage this creature leaves behind in its wake. There's no way I could possibly leave him to rot in this prison. Not when the only thing standing between us is a locked cell.

"All of them, Isla. Everything you've ever heard in town. You have to go."

I set my jaw. "No."

Rising from the floor, I reach into my cloak and

pull out the dagger I keep close to me at all times. It's not much, something Elyse swiped for me a few years ago, but it's gotten me out of more than a few sticky situations. I examine the door to the cell. It's a simple lock, and hope springs, in my chest. I could break it if I manage to get my dagger in there just right.

"Isla, leave," Father hisses, but I block him out.

I can do this. I *have* to do this. I'm bringing him home with me one way or another. I throw my weight into it, trying to snap the lock on the door somehow, but no matter how hard I tug, there's no give. "Dammit," I hiss, fighting the urge to scream. The urge to cry. He's right here, and there's nothing I can do to save him.

"Isla—"

Rage fills me, and I look Father in his eyes. "I'm not leaving you here, do you understand me? You're getting out of this prison."

But my hands cramp, and my muscles ache, and no matter how hard I tug and jerk, the door remains locked. He's so close, but so far away. A sob escapes me, and I throw the dagger aside, collapsing to my knees in front of Father. He reaches his hands forward to mine, lacing our fingers together. His touch makes me want to cry more. I should've been able to do this. I promised Elyse that I would.

"Sweetheart, you have to leave me. Please."

My throat clenches, and I press my forehead to the bars. Just as I start to speak, every hair on the back of my neck stands up.

"What do we have here?"

It's a voice that belongs to neither of us. It's rumbling, a low growl spoken through clenched teeth. My heart stops, and the blood in my veins turns to ice water. I spin around to find the source of the voice, and a strangled scream escapes my ragged throat.

It's him.

The Beast.

2

He's an abomination. He towers over Father and me, at least eight feet tall, maybe even nine. Tall enough to force him to hunch over just slightly, larger than the tiny, stifling room he's holding my father in.

Shrouded in the darkness, I can only see the outline of the creature, his chest broader than any human and his legs like the trunks of trees, heavy, expansive, and covered in a short coat of ashen fur. A hooded cloak covers his body and head, but I can feel his dark eyes staring holes through me even though I'm unable to see his face. The thought of what that must look like sends me shuddering, cowering against the metal bars of Father's prison.

"Please, Beast," Father pleads, rising from the floor. "My daughter knew no better. She only came to rescue me. But I've told her there's nothing she can do. I must own my mistakes and stay here. She was just leaving."

The creature's head cocks to the side, that rumbling growl growing even louder in the tight confines of the cellar. "She let herself into my home, the same as you." He drops a heavy foot forward as he approaches. "Like father, like daughter." There's some kind of twisted amusement in his voice that chills me to the core. The thoughts running through his mind must be sadistic, pleased that he's got us both in one place.

"I—I," I struggle to say, taking a shaky breath. "I'm sorry for coming here. I only thought he was in trouble."

"He is," the beast laughs. It's a mix between a snarl and a chuckle, a sound I consider a crime against nature. "He came into my home looking to take from me. Take my possessions for himself. Does he not know the consequences of theft in Graybrook?"

"He's old, sir," I say, slowly rising from the cement. "He's growing older every day. He was only trying to provide for me and my sister. But you have my word, whatever it is that he touched, my sister and I will pay for it. Everything he was going to take from you."

"No," the beast says, stepping closer. Close enough that I can feel the intense body heat radiating off of him. I try my hardest not to flinch, but I can't help myself. He's a wild animal in a room with us. At any moment, he could take my life.

"No, I've already given your father his punishment."

"What?" I ask. "What did you do to him?"

"He's not leaving these walls. He is mine, same as everything that steps foot in Highburn Hold."

My heart plummets, and I know now why Father wanted me to leave, to not involve myself in any of this. Even had I been able to get the lock open, he would've stayed in the cell. The beast would track us. Follow us home and slaughter us in our beds. All my efforts were in vain. There's no way that I could ever save him.

I spin around, facing him. "Tell me he's wrong, Papa," I beg.

Father's gaze has fallen. "He's not wrong, my love. I can't leave. I have to stay here."

"But, you're not well..."

He can't spend his final days here, rotting away in some monster's dungeon. I could never live with myself knowing that I'd left him down here to die while me and Elyse stayed safe at home.

"Take me," I say, turning to face the beast.

"Isla, no!" Father reaches through the bars, grabbing for my cloak. "Are you mad? You can't!"

"Take me instead," I tell the beast. "You don't want a sickly old man, do you? What's the fun in possessing him when I'm right here?"

It's twisted, but if this creature is still anything like the men I've known in life, there's no way he can turn this offer down. A young woman or her dying father. The choice is simple, and when the beast grunts and looks between us, I know that I've caught his attention. He's considering it, making his decision.

"No!" Father yells, tugging at the bars fruitlessly. "Beast, please. Don't! You have to let her go!"

"Quiet!"

The roar silences Father's pleas and forces me to take a step back, my heart skipping a beat in pure terror. To keep my brave face from falling, I stand up taller, staring directly into where I imagine the beast's eyes to be.

"You will stay here in place of your father?"

"Yes," I say, staring him down. "But you must let him return home. You cannot hurt him. If you let him go, I will stay. I'll be...yours."

It's a hopeless effort trying to make that statement sound confident and natural, but if he picks up any hesitation, the beast doesn't make it obvious.

"Mine," he repeats, and I can practically hear that toothy grin spread across his face. I shudder to imagine the sight.

"Isla, you can't," Father cries.

Without turning to him, I say, "I have. Go home, Father. Take care of Elyse. Tell her...tell her why I did this. That I love her."

"Come now, my beauty," the monster purrs, stretching out a hand. At least what I first imagine to be a hand. Rather, it's his...paw. Five fingerlike digits reach out for me, each with a thick black pad splayed around a larger pad where his palm should be. I reluctantly take his paw and let him pull me closer. His grip is tough, like worn weather gloves against my much smaller hand.

"Isla, please."

I finally turn back to Father and give him a somber smile. I don't want his last image of me to be one with tear-brimmed eyes and despair. "I love you," I tell him. Then I turn and follow the beast upstairs, leaving Father, the cellar, and my entire life behind me.

THE HALLS OF HIGHBURN HOLD ARE ALMOST OUT of a fairy tale; the kind of beauty my mother would tell me we would one day possess as she put me down for sleep. Luxurious paintings framed in gold. Mounted candles throwing shadows across the faces of the portraits on the walls. Lush rugs with intricate emerald and sapphire designs. Even the potted flowers seem to burst with a kind of vibrancy that just doesn't seem real.

It's fantastical, and it all makes me want to cry.

This place is a breathtaking prison, intentionally stunning to distract from the one sole fact that I may never leave these walls again.

The beast holds my hand in his and leads me through the winding halls. I try to steal a look at him, to know the face of the man who's captured me, but his silver cloak is long enough to cover him. We stop outside of a room, and with a quick twist, he opens it, pushing the door forward.

"This is where you will stay," he says. He gives me a firm push, and I step past the threshold, looking around the room. Just as the rest of the house was decorated with care, this place is decadence incarnate, with a massive, plush bed to one side, as well as an ornate wooden wardrobe, oak writing desk and chair, and a door that leads off into a personal lavatory.

"My father must leave that prison tonight," I tell the beast, turning around to face him. I have to angle my neck to look up at him, but I refuse to appear weak. I refuse to give him the satisfaction that I am now in his possession. "He must leave unharmed. I want a letter from him when he returns home, too."

"Are you in any position to make demands, my beauty?" His voice is cool, as if he's speaking to a small child. Dismissive in a way that makes me see red.

"If he's not taken care of and shown a way home, I will find a way to take my own life, and then you will have nothing." I don't know how I'll make it happen, but I will. He won't get to harm Father and keep me in his clutches.

"The old man will return home safely. Meanwhile, you will remain within these walls for as long as I see fit. Punishment for your filthy father's attempted theft."

"You have more than enough to share," I challenge.

A rumbling from the beast echoes off the stone walls. "I do not share what is mine."

His possessiveness turns my stomach. It's almost comforting to know that arrogance and entitlement aren't traits exclusive to males of the human variety. Even a great and terrible beast such as the one before me has his shortcomings.

"I will come to find you when it's time for you to leave the room. Until then, you will have servants at your disposal. Food at your fingertips. You will remain presentable. Remember that you are my possession, beauty, and I will not allow my things to appear unpleasant."

I want to strike him. I nod instead. "Okay. What should I call you?"

"Beast," he says. "The same way everyone else does."

"Okay, Beast," I say. "I have one more request."

He tenses up like I've overstepped a bit too far. "What?"

"Show me... Show me your face."

The beast hesitates for a moment, standing as still as a furry statue. After a brief silence, he raises his paws to his hood and pulls it free, revealing the monster beneath. It's startling to see such a creature, with his lion-like head, protruding snout, downward curved white horns, and startlingly human eyes. They seem to glow an unnatural shade of yellow, a stark contrast to his wolfish gray coloring. His brows are heavy and low, expressive in a way, and in the light, I'm able to see the black claws as they retract into his paws. His dark lips part as he says,

"Are you afraid?"

I'm not afraid.

It's not fear that burns through me.

I don't know *what* it is. Curiosity? A desire to see

more of him, to understand this bastardized amalgamation of nature? I crave the knowledge of how this happened, how such a thing could be born into the world. These thoughts race through my mind all at once, confusing me. But I know for certain that I'm not afraid of him. At least, not in this moment.

"No," I say, meeting his glowing eyes. "You don't scare me."

"Just wait," he says. "Maybe not now. Maybe not tomorrow. But soon."

"Give me something to be afraid of, and perhaps I will."

The tiniest smirk tugs on his lips as he reaches for the door. "You will have food brought to you tomorrow morning. Get some sleep tonight."

It's not a suggestion, judging from his tone of voice. After the way I've spoken to him tonight, I don't dare press my luck any further. Rather, I nod and say, "Sleep well." He pauses, eyes narrowed on me for a tense moment. It's as if he wants to say something, but instead of speaking, he closes the door. The twist of a lock follows shortly after.

Only when he's gone do I let my shoulders sink. I drag myself to the bed, the weight of my situation pressing down on me. It buckles my knees and breaks my back. I don't know what I've gotten myself into. Do I regret this? Would I rather Father be the one held captive in Beast's castle? Never. The knowledge that this was the one way to save him is the only thing that keeps me from choking up. He spent his life sacrificing for Elyse and me. This is the reprieve he deserves.

Curling into a small ball on the monumental bed, I reach for the soft sheets and pull them over my body, resting my head on the pillow. I don't know what will come of this, but I'm certain that in my dreams, nothing can hurt me.

3

Two weeks. Fourteen days. It's been maddening remaining in the same room. I'm practically crawling up the walls. The beast refuses to let me out no matter how much I plead. I don't have to leave Highburn, but I need to stretch my legs. I need fresh air. And still, he refuses.

Tells me that his word is law and that when the time is right, he will let me leave the room. All I can do is pray that this day will come soon. I'm not sure I can retain my sanity for much longer if this goes any further.

When the sun pokes over the hills and illuminates my bedroom, I fight the urge to hide beneath my blankets. I want to sleep this entire day away. In my sleep, I'm not confined to one room. I can mount a horse and take off in the middle of the night, leaving behind the beast and this horrible, beautiful place once and for all.

A few moments pass before there's a knock at the door. A twist of a lock follows, and Mrs. Potter enters the room. She's an older woman, close to fifty or so, with a smile that's been my only source of comfort. She comes bearing food on a silver tray: a bowl of porridge with berries, bread, tea, and a handful of strawberries in a side dish.

"Good morning, dear," she says, carrying the tray to me. "I hope you slept well."

Truth be told, I didn't, but she's been so kind to me that I lie and say, "Like a baby," offering her a kind smile in return. "This looks delicious, Mrs. Potter. Thank you."

She waves a frail hand in the air. "Don't thank me. It's my job."

"Still," I say, insisting. "Thank you. Will you join me for breakfast?"

Mrs. Potter's lips purse as she considers it. "I probably shouldn't. Mister Lovell wouldn't want me sitting down while I have work to do."

I tilt my head and say, "I won't say a word to him if you won't."

We exchange a conspiratorial smile before Mrs. Potter sits beside me. We share toast and berries while she tells me of her grandson's accomplishments.

He's been struggling in his studies, his attention pulled in a million different directions, but he's finally begun to enjoy reading, and now every night after her work here in Highburn, the two of them read in the study.

"If you would like to join us, you're more than welcome to," she offers.

The idea is a sharp slap in the face. "I can't," I whisper, the oatmeal souring in my stomach. "The beast refuses to let me out. I don't know if I'll ever be free of this room, Mrs. Potter. But I desperately want to. To explore, to read with you and your grandson..."

A swell of heartache cuts my words short, and I turn my head, allowing a lock of hair to cover my face. I don't need this woman to see me cry. The least I can do is appreciate her kindness while she's here with me.

"Darling," she says, reaching for my hand. "He'll let you out soon. He has...preparations to make."

"What kind of preparations?" I turn back to face her, wiping my eyes with my free hand.

"It's been so long since he's had a guest in his home. At least one that isn't in the cellar. Mister Lovell is a prideful man. He requires everything to be spotless. Pristine. And he wants it to be beautiful for you."

I don't know whether to feel touched or wary. It's

kind of him to care about the image of his castle, but how kind can he be if he's still my captor? How much compassion can I reserve for him when he would've just as easily allowed my father to rot in his prison?

"I just don't know how much more of this I can bear, Mrs. Potter," I say, brushing dark brown hair behind my ears. "I've been here so long, and I still know nothing. Not his name. Not his story. The only thing I know for certain is that he's controlling and cruel. The kind of person to have a jail in his home."

She nods somberly. "Mister Lovell can be...difficult. And quite controlling. The servants here aren't allowed to leave more than a few times every year. He's strict with the rules, and God forbid we break those rules. I've seen cooks permanently scarred for preparing his meat incorrectly."

My eyes bulge with fear, and I shiver at the thought. The claws hidden beneath skin and fur must be enormous. The damage he could do to a person...

"He's horrible," I cry.

"Now, now," she says, pulling me into her arms. "He has his faults, but Isla...he's not all bad."

"How can someone like him *not* be?"

"He has his moments of kindness. When my Charlie climbed up a tree to see the town down below, he couldn't get down. Mister Lovell talked him down. Got him to climb low enough to jump. And when he broke down in tears, Mister Lovell held him and let him cry."

I don't want to discount Mrs. Potter's story, but that man can't possibly cohabitate the same evil form of the man I met weeks before. There's no way a beast that vile could have a tender side to him. But I don't dare speak ill of him. Not any more than I already have. Instead, I ask,

"What happened to him? Was he...born that way?"

Mrs. Potter smiles. "No, he was quite handsome once. But that was his undoing." She looks over her shoulder to make sure the door is still closed before she leans in close. "There are many stories about how he ended up in this condition. Magic gone awry. Demons. A particularly nasty rumor about his mother and her favorite bloodhound. But it was the curse."

"The curse?" I don't mean to sound so enthusiastic, but after spending a fortnight alone with my thoughts, I take to this idea like a moth to flame.

"It's been some time since it happened. Almost ten years, I believe. There was a woman looking for shelter during a terrible storm. She came to the house and begged to be let in, just for the night. Mister Lovell turned her and her young daughter away."

My stomach twists at the thought. I knew he was

heartless. Beyond the ability to speak and those golden eyes, there's no humanity left in him.

"The woman's daughter, unfortunately, didn't make it through the night. She turned blue in her mother's arms." Mrs. Potter's eyes fall, and she takes a slow breath. "The woman returned to Highburn and demanded to see Mister Lovell. When he finally came to see him, she blew something in his face. Something that left him coughing and choking on the floor. We tried taking him to his room to recover, but when we returned the following morning, we found a monster laying beneath his sheets."

"It's what he deserved," I say without thinking.

Mrs. Potter says, "I wish he'd learned his lesson from her. It was punishment for being so cold to her, turning him into the kind of monster that would put out a child in need. For a long time, he hid himself away, refusing to let us see what he looked like. He was horrified with himself and so very, very violent. As the years went by, he slowly opened back up. He's no kinder than he was then, but he speaks with us once more."

It feels impossible to imagine Beast being worse than he was the night I found my father in his cellar, but I believe her. A man as wealthy and standoffish as he must've been could very easily become violent after what that sorceress did to him.

"Did you ever see that woman again?" I ask.

"Never. He sent men to go find her, but she was gone as if she disappeared entirely. We never even found the body of her daughter. That only made him more enraged. But time has calmed him down. Helped him settle. He's not the same person he was when it first happened, thankfully."

The silence between us is heavy, and I thank Mrs. Potter for spending the morning with me. Almost regretfully, she takes my tray and locks the door behind herself when she leaves. Now that I'm alone again, I can't help but think about the beast and his history.

From what Mrs. Potter says, he was once a terrible man, abusing his servants and leaving children out in the cold to freeze to death. But at the same time, he's helpful to her grandson Charlie, and he's brought me up to this room rather than keeping me locked in the prison down below. It's as if all of his negatives come with something positive, an ounce of humanity that, to me, seems almost uncharacteristic.

I hate that I've thought so much about him. I hate him more than I hate that. I just want to be free. To see Father and Elyse and be home with them as Father spends his final weeks with us. Instead, I'm a caged bird in this exquisite castle. A rose beneath glass, suffocating as its petals wither and fall free. Once again, I consider the window. That is until there's another knock at the door.

A man enters, one I've never seen before, and I cover myself with the sheets, unwilling to let him see me in my undergarments. To my relief, he doesn't even toss a glance my way. He carries in a gorgeous gown and a small white piece of paper. He places them both on the writing desk, walks out, and locks the door once more.

Hesitantly curious, I inch toward the desk and look down at the paper.

My Beauty,

Tonight, you will join me for dinner. I will send Eleanor to help dress you. I would like you to wear this gown. It has been specially made for you. I hope that you find it as pleasing as I do.

I scrunch my face up and reach for the gown, lifting it from the wooden table. It's simple yet beautiful, made with soft dandelion silk and a neckline that scoops down to expose the collarbones. The sleeves stop just below the elbow, where the material ruffles, giving shape to the otherwise standard silhouette. It's beautiful, but I don't want it.

I want none of his gifts.

I want to leave.

But I'm not a child. I know that he won't let me. The best I can do is remind myself of the lessons my mother taught me. When life was hard, and Father struggled to provide for us, she taught me and Elyse to make the best of what we had. To always find the positives. To always look to the sunshine, rather than the shadows.

So, I carry the dress to my bed and lay it down. It's not the worst gift I've ever received. It must have been expensive to make, and he had it created for me. Of course, it's to have dinner with him in, but regardless.

"It's dinner," I tell myself, tracing my fingers over the fabric. "Just dinner. You can do this."

I'm not certain if I can. I just know that I must.

4

The sun just starts to set when Mrs. Potter arrives to help me get dressed. I feel bad for how much work she has to do around the house, but I appreciate her company. She's quickly become my best—and only—friend here at Highburn Hold.

It takes a while to finish, but when I'm all dressed and my hair is styled up into a regal bun, Mrs. Potter says, "My goodness," with her hand over her chest.

Bashfully, I fiddle with some of the silk on my gown. "Thank you, Mrs. Potter."

"Don't thank me. I'm happy that I got to do this for you. Now, we best not keep Mister Lovell waiting. Come, come."

I follow her down the long hall leading to the grand staircase. My stomach roils with anxiety. I'm almost too nauseous to eat. And while nerves threaten to ruin my appetite, I'm also excited to see more of the castle. Being cooped up for so long is no way to live.

Beast stands at the bottom of the staircase in a suit. For a moment, I'm certain I've fallen asleep and dreamed this all up. But there he is, dressed elegantly in a blue suit that has to have been custom-made. He raises his hand for me, and I force a small smile when I descend close enough to take it.

His hold on me is light, and it's a quick reminder that before he became what he is tonight, he was once a wealthy man who undoubtedly took all kinds of etiquette classes. He knows how to treat a woman with respect. At least on paper.

I don't feel very respected, having finally been let out of my bedroom after two weeks.

"You look lovely," he says, leading me through the door to the dining room.

"Thank you," I say, looking him over. "You look... handsome, Beast." I must be mistaken because I see what appears to be a smile on his face. But just as quickly, he stops walking and gestures to what is set up in front of us.

I can't remember the last time I've ever seen so much food on a table. Roast meats, vegetables, side dishes, and desserts take up nearly every inch of the dining table, practically as far as the eye can see. It's far too much for two people, but I say nothing. Instead, I let Beast lead me to my chair, watching as he pulls it out for me.

Yet another peculiar thing about this...animal.

He rounds the table to sit across from me. "I'm glad you decided to join me, Isla," he says.

"I'm not sure I had very much of a choice," I reply, trying to keep my voice light. I'd be foolish to say no after hearing all of the things he's done to those that upset him. I'd rather not end up scarred like his cooks.

If he heard my reply, he ignores it, continuing with, "I had my cooks prepare everything. I wasn't sure what you might like, so I figured you could choose once you got here." He gives a quick clap, and two servants appear from behind me, walking around the table and explaining all of my options.

It leaves my mind spinning, all the food he's had prepared. When they reach the end of the table, I decide on a bit of roast lamb, potatoes, and a thick piece of bread. Something filling enough to keep me held over until breakfast in the morning. While they serve me, Beast clears his throat.

"I'm sorry that I was unable to let you out sooner. I wanted it all to be perfect."

"Why?" I ask without thinking.

A strange look crosses his face. "What do you mean, 'why'?"

"It's just... I'm not your guest. I'm your...what did you call it? Your possession?"

He hums quietly, thoughtfully, and nods. "You are. But I wasn't raised in poverty. I have manners. Particularly when it comes to women."

"How romantic," I murmur, picking at my potato absently. My appetite isn't present, but I know that it will upset him if I don't eat. In his eyes, it might seem rude or unappreciative. So, I scoop up a bite of food and chew, staring at those haunting eyes from across the cavernous room. "Am I allowed out of my room now?"

"You are. There are certain rooms here that are locked, but beyond those, Highburn Hold is your home as well. The gardens. The libraries. You're welcome to explore. Within reason, of course."

"Of course."

"But it comes with a price, my beauty."

The way he says it, I feel my stomach clench, and I raise my gaze to his. Even sitting so far away, I can feel something radiating off of him. When Father tried to teach me and Elyse how to hunt, I felt that same buzz of energy. He's a predator, watching my every move and waiting for a chance to strike. He's made me his prey.

"What is the price, Beast?"

"You will be mine. In every way."

An uncontrollable smile appears on my face, and I cover my mouth with my hand. Impossible. He's not asking...asking me for that. Is he? No, he has to understand that I would never. I *could* never. Not only is he a mistake of a man, but also of mankind. The product of apathy, of self-serving arrogance, not a viable option for intimacy.

"I'm sorry," I say, stifling my laughter as best I can. "I don't...I don't mean to."

"Do you find something amusing?"

"You were being serious?" That's when the laughter dies down. I reach for my water and take a long sip. I hate that my hand shakes when I return the cup to the table. "Beast, I don't think I can."

His brows lower, and he narrows his eyes at me. "What do you mean? Of course, you can. You are mine, and I've decided this for us."

"You don't get to make that decision for me," I say, my voice dropping. "When I eat, when I leave, fine. But not that. Never that."

With a sudden outburst of rage, he knocks his cup and silver tray to the floor, splattering the stone with wet heaps of food. He pushes himself from his chair, chest heaving in anger. My immediate instinct is to run. To avoid this wild animal like my life depends on it. It very well might.

"You do not tell me what I can and cannot have, Isla. If I want you as mine and mine alone, that's what you will be." He stalks toward me, his massive form growing larger as he approaches. "After I've been generous to gift you with the gown you wear. The meals you eat. The bed you lay your head upon. I've even spared your pathetic father's life. I gave him the chance to die with pride. And yet you believe you can tell me no?"

My heart pounds in my chest, so loud I'm sure he can hear it, and I stand on wobbling knees, looking for assistance from the servants. They stand with hands clasped behind their backs, eyes trained on the floor.

"One thing you will learn, my beauty, is that if I want something, I will have it."

I dive for the blade on the table, pulling it from the roast and brandishing it toward him. "Don't you dare..." I warn him. He looks down at the knife, which to him must seem like a needle, and he scoffs.

"Do you truly think you could hurt me, Isla? A fragile little thing like yourself?"

I quickly weigh the options. If I try to hurt him, I'll have to be lucky enough to kill him in one quick motion. I don't think I've been blessed with that kind of fortune. Instead, I press the blade into the side of my neck.

He freezes in place, eyes growing wide. "What are you doing?"

"I was told you were a man with many qualities. Bad and good. But if being here, being yours, means that you will do with me whatever you wish, then I'd rather die. I'd rather bleed out on this floor than let something like you defile me in any way."

Impossibly, it's as if my words have hit deeper than any knife I could've pushed into him would be able to. That familiar grumbling finds its way to my ears, and his nostrils flare, chest rapidly rising and falling as his anger builds and builds. I press the blade deeper into my skin, piercing it enough to draw blood. It runs down my neck gradually, but still, I keep the pressure, never once faltering.

"Would you rather have your possession living or dead, Beast?" I ask. He starts forward, and before his large foot can land, I press the blade deeper, whimpering as it sinks into my skin more. "Tell me," I order.

Anger tears through him again, and he grips the table, flipping it with so much force that it lifts from the ground, tumbling through the air before it connects with the wall. The servants just barely duck out of the way, scrambling to the kitchen and out of sight.

With the candles on the table extinguished, we're submerged in darkness. Before I can react, there's a paw on my hand, yanking the knife from my neck. I struggle with him, but he's much too strong. His breath is hot on my neck, and in a soft, ominous voice, he says,

"Do not ever hurt yourself again." I try to jerk free, but he adds more pressure to my wrist. At any moment, he could snap it beneath his grip. "Never again. Do you understand?" Beast shoves me to the side, sending me stumbling.

Though I can't see much more than his hulking silhouette, he pushes through the doors of the dining room, leaving them open as he climbs the stairs. It isn't until he's out of sight that I finally breathe. I collapse to my knees, holding my hand over the wound on my neck carefully. It burns, but I didn't go deep enough to do any permanent damage.

What hurts more is the tightness of my throat. The terror pumping through me. He could've hurt me, but he didn't. He could've let me take my own life, but he didn't. I don't know what to make of any of this.

Blood seeps through my fingers, and I rise from my knees, heading to the kitchen. There, I find the servants from before whispering. They stop the moment I enter the spacious room.

"Are you okay, Isla?" the man asks, rushing toward me to examine the wound. "Did he hurt you anywhere else?"

"No," I say, starting to shake my head but wincing. "I don't know why."

"I don't either," he says in a curious tone. "Here, let me get someone to help take care of this." He sits me down at a table in the back of the kitchen and hurries away. When he returns, there's a woman with him, a few years older than Mrs. Potter, and she sits beside me, pushing hair behind my ear to get a better look at the wound.

"You're lucky you only got away with just this," she says in a hollow, exhausted tone. "I've seen folks walk away with much worse scars."

"He didn't lay a hand on me. I did this."

She nods slowly. "Of course not. He wouldn't want to damage his beauty."

I can't explain why, but that fills me with fire. I'm not his object. I'm not the prize some bastard creature won in a game. But she's right. He didn't hurt me because he wouldn't want to damage me. The fact that he withheld his temper is evidence enough that he still wants to control me. Control how I look for him.

I'm too tired to reach for the knife and scar myself more, but the thought crosses my mind. I hate him more than I've ever hated anyone before. More than I hated God when He struck my father down with his illness. More than I hated Him when He took my mother from me.

But my body shuts down, and I ease into the chair, allowing this woman to patch me up and tend to my self-inflicted wound. My eyelids grow heavy, and soon, the darkness of sleep graciously comes to take me.

5

Truly, I expected some kind of punishment for my behavior at dinner. The beast doesn't immediately strike me as the kind to forget so easily. But in an odd turn of events, there have been no consequences. He leaves my bedroom door unlocked. We have our meals together in the dining hall. We don't talk much, but I'm cordial, out of fear more than anything else. I'm waiting for something to happen, ears perked up, trying to detect any danger.

But Beast is either playing the long game with me, teasing his prey before he kills me, or he's simply...not going to do anything about it.

Mrs. Potter was scared when she saw my wound the next morning, and eventually, she pried the information out of me. "Oh, dear, I don't know if that was such a good idea," she told me.

"I don't care," I said, headstrong. "He wanted to... to... I'm not even sure what he wanted from me. Marriage? Sex? I will give him neither, and I will make sure he can never take the choice from me. I'd rather die a thousand deaths."

She seemed as if she wanted to speak, but I'd already made up my mind.

Whether Beast had intended to make me his bride or his whore that night, I don't know. The only thing I'm sure of is that I was lucky. Father always told me that I was the smartest girl he knew. Always thinking on my feet, always surviving. It's clear that if I'm going to spend time in this place, I have to survive. Never let my guard down. Never give Beast the chance.

Thankfully, since that night one week ago, he's refrained from even mentioning what happened. It's an elephant in the room, nearly the size of his massive form, and we pretend it isn't there.

As dinnertime approaches, I sort through some of the dresses he's given me since I came to stay with him. There's a stunning blue one that I've become quite fond of, and when Mrs. Potter arrives in my room to help me get dressed, I hand it to her.

"How are you feeling, dear? Has the wound on your neck finally healed?"

I step into the gown and nod. "It has. I think it might leave a permanent scar, though."

"Mm," she says simply.

I look over my shoulder at her as she laces me into the dress. "What's on your mind?"

"Nothing, nothing," she says, waving her hand through the air. But after a moment of uncomfortable silence, she adds, "It's just that Mister Lovell won't like that."

"I don't care what he likes," I say defiantly. That's not entirely true. I know he doesn't like when I sass him or show any form of insubordination, and I've done a good job not upsetting him or riling him up since that night.

"You're a brave girl, Isla."

I can't help but smile. It's obvious she's replaced her real thoughts with the word 'brave.' I'm going to take the compliment anyway, though. To volunteer for my father, and sacrifice my own life for his, takes bravery. Imprudence, too, but bravery nonetheless.

"After dinner, I think I will go for a walk through the gardens," I say absently.

"You should. They're most beautiful during the winter."

That's something I never thought I would hear. In

Graybrook, like most places, winter is a time for hibernation. Trees lose their leaves and flowers their lives, but not in the gardens of Highburn Hold. Impossibly, the property here has managed to retain the lives of all the shrubbery. Outside the walls of the castle, near the forest, there are flowers. Bright, healthy, thriving flowers. My favorite are the roses, where they climb the walls and surround a comfortable wooden bench. The contrast is beautiful in its own way.

All through dinner, the rose garden is the one thing on my mind. I make small conversation with Beast, but he seems as standoffish as ever, trying to dazzle me with various wines and desserts that have come from all over the world when the one thing I want the most is to be among his flowers. Finally, after we share a piece of cake, he ends dinner.

I gather my skirt and bound up the stairs, grabbing a thick fur cloak from my bedroom. It takes a good five minutes to make it through the winding maze of greenery, but I finally arrive, holding a hand over my heart. I want to capture this place in my memory forever. I want to, when the weather grows warmer, bring books out here and enjoy the smell of the flowers as I read.

If I knew I wouldn't get in trouble, I'd collapse right here in a bed of pansies and laugh myself silly.

Instead, I run my fingers over flower petals, their softness kissing my fingertips as I walk through the breathtaking display of skillful horticulture.

I let out a sharp hiss and tug my hand away, bringing it to my chest. When I examine it, I can see a large bead of blood on the tip. One of the thorns from the roses. The droplet falls from my finger and hits the snow, spattering.

"Look, but don't touch," I say to the bushes of flowers. "Noted."

I continue deeper into the garden, keeping the forest on my left and my finger in my mouth, tasting the bitter, metallic flavor of my blood. It's not pleasant, but it's certainly not the worst thing in the world, either. Lost in thought, I end up standing at the forest's edge, staring into the darkness of the woods.

Without thinking, one foot moves in front of the other, leading me through the trees. I could run away right here and now. I could just take off, leave everything behind, and make it home. Tell Father and Elyse to pack up and move out of Graybrook. It would be easy to disappear. We've done it in the past.

The thought of running away leads me deeper into the woods, and my heart pounds with every step I move. The excitement is so overwhelming that I miss the rustling around me until it's far too late. All at once, I hear low growls and see glowing eyes. I freeze in place, terror sinking my stomach down to the soles of my feet as I watch the wolves convene in front of me.

Their teeth are bared, and their bloodlust practically radiates like heat waves. They're hungry, and it looks like they've just found their prey.

I bend down to grab a rock and toss it at the shaggy gray wolf in front, knocking it in the head. "Go away," I warn them. It shakes off the injury and snaps its teeth at me, inching closer. "No!" I yell, throwing another small rock. This time, the wolf sidesteps it and lunges for me.

I barely have time to dodge it when the rest shoot toward me. I let out a scream and turn around, scrambling in the opposite direction. I can feel them on my heels, snapping at me, desperate to tear into me the same way I'm desperate to evade them. I don't even have it in me to scream. Not when I need to save my energy for my escape.

There's a searing pain in my leg, so bright that it takes me a moment to realize that one of them has just clamped down on my thigh. I cry out and pound my fist against the animal's head until it releases me. Another dives for my neck, but I take off running again, limping as my weight makes the injury more noticeable.

I just barely break through the line of trees before my knees give out, and I trip forward, plummeting into the snow. I roll onto my side and watch the wolves close in, my body frozen in place. It's over. They'll have their meal after all.

A deafening roar sends a shiver through my spine and makes my teeth rattle, but it doesn't come from the pack moving in on me. It's deeper, like it's vibrating, from within the ground. Heavier, with more bass. Seconds later, I see the large shape of Beast bounding toward us, down on all fours, putting himself between me and the wolves. The betas step back in fear, but not the alpha. The alpha is defiant, snarling at Beast, baring its teeth once more. Beast growls again, lowering his stance, muscles visible beneath taut fur. He's an animal, same as them, but he's bigger. Stronger.

The alpha doesn't back down, and instead, moving like lightning, it jumps toward Beast. He's faster, and I let out a gasp as he catches the creature by the throat, squeezing hard enough that I can hear the snap of its neck. Lazily, he tosses the wolf to its pack, where they whine and nudge their fallen leader.

Beast lowers himself to the ground once more and roars at them hard enough to send them running with their tails between their legs. When he's sure they won't return, he rises and turns to face me. The snarl etched into his face startles me, and he licks at his dagger-sharp teeth hungrily. All at once, his body relaxes, powerful muscles loosening as his face softens. I don't know what to say, and thankfully, I don't have to be the one to break the silent tension.

He takes hold of my hand and pulls me up. "Are you okay?" he asks, concern now replacing the rage in his eyes.

With a shaky breath, I say, "I'm okay. Just a bite. It didn't go too deep." I try to show that I'm fine, but when I step, my injured leg buckles, and I nearly collapse.

"Here. Let me help you."

I don't protest when Beast scoops me up from the ground like I weigh nothing. He brings me close to his chest, cradling me against him as he begins to walk. I expect him to smell like a mutt, but he doesn't. He smells clean, a slightly masculine aroma from the soap he's used. Pressed this close to him, I also feel warmer than any cloak or shawl has ever made me feel.

He looks down at me. "Why were you so far out? Were you trying to run?"

Everything in me screams to lie. Make up some excuse that won't be grounds for punishment. But he's just saved my life. The least he's owed is my honesty. "Yes. Not at first, but being in the woods... I wanted to leave."

"Is being in my home less desirable than the wolves of these woods?"

He's hurt. I can tell by the way his face goes blank. He's hiding his emotions, trying to make it appear like he's unbothered, but spending the past few weeks with him, I know that it does. It must eat away at him to know that the only person in his home that he doesn't pay so clearly dislikes him. Avoids him during the day and only interacts with him when she must.

My silence must be answer enough because he adds, "I'm sorry."

"For what?"

"For making you think that death was a better option than living here. With me." His eyes never leave the trail back to the castle, which only makes me feel even more anxious. Is this sincere, or is he using his words to manipulate me into getting what he wants?

"I appreciate what you do for me, Beast. I want you to know that I do. I've never had meals more delicious than the ones you have prepared for me. But you scare me. Your anger scares me. Can you imagine being in my position?"

His eyes fall to meet mine, brow bone sloping up in concentration. "What position is that?"

"If you felt like it, you could have me killed. Or worse. You could overpower me with ease. And there's nothing I could do to stop you from hurting me. All the gowns and sweets and jewelry in the world would never be enough to make me forget that."

"I would never hurt you, Isla."

"So you say."

His mouth presses into a thin line, and while my instinct is to offer him sympathy, he must understand what I'm saying. He knows nothing of the danger I'm in. The danger women are in around men with his temperament. His whole life, he's been in power, in possession of the kind of wealth that makes him untouchable. Of course, he would struggle to see the world through my eyes. It doesn't matter how crest-fallen he is. He must hear it.

"If it's company that you wish to have, you must be good company yourself. Not a man that throws tables and threatens to force his wishes on those around him, but a man that values people. I'm mine before I'm ever yours," I say. There's no unease in my voice. No room for negotiation. He will never imply that I owe him anything in exchange for gifts he's given of his own free will. I am not indebted to this man, but rather enslaved.

"And when will you be mine?" he asks.

"When I choose."

Beast gives a short nod but says nothing more. I can tell that he wants to argue, but thankfully, he's not opened his mouth again. Grateful to have silence, I turn into him, pressing my face against the solid muscle of his chest, and close my eyes. The pain in my leg hasn't gone down, but my adrenaline has. I can finally breathe without worrying about the pack of wolves from before. As I settle in his hold, a soft, purring noise rumbles in his body. I don't dare point it out, but I've heard that noise with cats before.

It's a purr of approval. I wonder if he knows he's doing it or if it's something beyond his control. I know, without doubt, that he likes this, though. My body against his. The opportunity to protect me and bring me home. It's what he's wanted since the beginning.

Stranger yet, I think that I might like the feeling of this as well.

❧ 6 ❧

Eating dinner alone is something I never imagined would be so unnerving, yet here I sit, quietly chewing lamb as the servants stand to the side of the room, watching. Waiting for instruction. It's strange. All my life, I'd been told stories that one day, there would be feasts awaiting me and Elyse. Now that I have them, I'm not quite sure I like them all that much.

I wish the servants wouldn't stand so uncomfortably silent, but instead of voicing this, I say, "Please, have a seat."

The man, Henry, looks at me fearfully. "What?"

"Both of you. Join me. I can't possibly eat all of this alone."

Henry and the woman, Eva, share a glance. She

clears her throat. "We can't, Miss. Mister Lovell doesn't allow us to eat. Not while we are working."

"Beast isn't here," I tell them. I don't know where he is, but he's decided to skip dinner. He's broken one of the few agreements we've made—that we enjoy our meals together—so it's only fair that I'm allowed to do the same.

"I don't think that's a good idea, Miss." Though Eva speaks with conviction, I see her eyeing the grand spread of food longingly.

"Eva. Henry. If he has something to say, I will address it with him. But I can't enjoy my food with you two standing there hungry. Please. You would be helping me out, which is what Beast wants you to do."

There's a long, heavy moment of silence between them before finally, Henry steps out of the room. He returns with two chairs. Eva sets the trays down for them, and I smile as they begin to prepare their meal.

As we eat, we make small conversation. Eva and Henry have been married for thirteen years. They began working for Beast's family when his father, Gregor, ran into them at a small bar in the village. He paid double what they were making there. When he died, Beast kept them employed, though his payments grew noticeably smaller.

I stifle my anger when I hear this news. Mrs.

Potter said that he's gotten better, but the more I hear about his behavior from the past, the more upset I become. The way he's treated everyone in his life, from his staff to his captives... It's unacceptable.

After dinner, I help Henry and Eva clear the table, still confused as to why Beast decided not to come down to eat. We make quick work of the trays and utensils, cleaning them and disposing of what food we didn't eat. What can be preserved is stored safely while the rest is thrown out.

I dry my hands and make my way for the stairs when I pause, hand on the banister. I don't know what it is, but something tells me to go looking for Beast. It's unlike him to miss dinner. In the weeks that I've been at Highburn, he's never missed a meal.

I climb the stairs in search of him, knocking on his bedroom door when I arrive. Poking my head in, I don't find him inside. As my search through the castle continues, I find myself growing more worried. Has something happened to him? Is he well?

Hurrying down a long corridor, I slow my gait when I see a flicker of light outside. It's coming from the gardens. Beast is kneeling, head down, unmoving. A chill of fear surges through me, and I turn on my heels, hurrying downstairs. I push through the doors and race to the garden, breathless by the time I make it to the frozen fountain.

Beast hasn't moved an inch, and as I step closer, I hear him murmuring something.

"...I'm trying. Every day. But I don't know what to do. How to fix any of this."

There's pain in his voice. A kind of hurt men don't allow themselves to express around just anyone. I consider reaching out to him, offering him a comforting touch, but remain frozen in place. He steps back, and that's when I see it.

He's been kneeling in front of a grave marked Rose Lovell.

Beside it, just visible, behind Beast's profile, is one for Gregor.

These were his parents. He was talking to his parents, and I've just interrupted this moment. I take a step back to leave, and rather than my foot planting, it shoots forward, the patch of ice beneath my shoes throwing me off-balance. I fall onto my behind with a heavy thud. Beast's head snaps in my direction, ears pointed toward me, eyes ablaze with awareness.

"Sorry," I say, scrambling up to dust the snow from my dress. "I... I was just..."

"You shouldn't be here," he growls. "You should be in your room."

"I know," I say, lacing my fingers together and shifting uneasily on my feet. "I'm sorry. I just thought something might be wrong. You—you didn't come to dinner."

"I have no appetite," he says. "Not today." His head swivels back to the grave, and he presses his forehead to the cool stone.

"When did it happen?" I ask. I take a tentative step closer. It's clear that he wants me gone so he can deal with this alone, but when Mother passed, I said I wanted solitude when what I needed was community. I needed Elyse, and Father, and the people in the village that consoled me in various ways. Isolation was the last thing that would have helped me.

"Go," he mutters. "Go back inside."

Disobeying him, I step closer, inch by inch, until I'm able to kneel down beside him. The chill of the snow cuts through my dress almost immediately, but the cold doesn't bother me. Instead, I place my hand on his large forearm.

"Beast," I say lightly. "Tell me. I want to know."

Almost reluctantly, he glances at me. "Seventeen years ago. I was just a boy. Fifteen. She fell ill, and a few months later, she was gone."

"I'm sorry you had to go through that."

"Don't be. I hated her for so long," he spits out. "She got to leave while I was stuck with him."

The lack of attention he's paid to Gregor's gravestone is noticeable. He doesn't even look at it when he talks about his father. I don't know what to say to him because his life is still shrouded in mystery. It would only be performative were I to try and offer him some kind of encouraging speech.

"I realized when I was older that she was stuck with him the same way I was. Had it not been for my birth, she would have run. She would've left my father and all his money to get away from him. You say that I'm frightening, Isla, but you've never met him."

Finally, Beast turns to stare at Gregor's grave as he says, "I'm not the proof that monsters exist in this world. The body lying in that grave is. The way he treated my mother. The ways he hurt her. Humiliated her. It took me years to realize that the reason I hated her wasn't because she died, but because in death, she surely found relief."

Shamefully, I regret thinking, even for a moment, that Gregor was better than his son. If even half of what Beast has implied is true, then I'm thankful I've never met Gregor Lovell before.

"I'm sorry you had to go through that with him," I say, stroking through his fur.

Beast turns to look at me again, head-on, his brow bone contorted into concern. "What is your father like?" he asks.

This is the first time he's brought Father up since

he insulted him for doing what he needed to do to take care of his family. I'm hesitant to mention it because I don't want to upset Beast again, but he doesn't look like he's going to drop the subject any time soon. I take a slow breath.

"He's a good man. Selfless. Caring. He's taken care of me and my sister Elyse since Mother passed away. I'm sure you don't see him as such, but he's a hard worker."

"He's a thief," Beast says.

"And you're a kidnapper. I've stolen before. So has my sister. We only take what we need from those that have excess." I give him a pointed look. If he gave away even a fraction of what he had, he could improve the lives of so many families. I do not see the point in amassing a large wealth if not to give to those who need the assistance.

Beast clears his throat. "I suppose I shouldn't judge. Your father never hit you or your mother."

"Never," I say, frowning at the thought of Beast as a child, fearful of the man whose job it was to protect him. I don't know what he looked like, but I imagine a blond boy.

"I don't apologize for what I did, Isla. I found him breaking into my home. He's lucky I didn't have him killed," he starts. "But, I apologize for the way I treated him."

"It doesn't matter," I say, shaking my head. "You let him go home, and that's all that matters. That's all I wanted. If I have to spend time here in his place, then I don't care. Just as long as he's home safe."

Thinking about him makes me sad, and I sniff hard, refusing to cry at the thought of being back with him. I know that Elyse is taking care of him. He's safe in bed, and that's what helps calm me down when I start to get anxious. I must remind myself why it is that I've found myself in this gilded prison with this cursed man and his anger problems.

"You should go back inside. You're shivering," Beast suggests.

"I'm okay. I want to be here with you."

He frowns and shakes his head. "I don't understand you."

"What's not to understand?"

"One minute, you want nothing to do with me. You tell me I terrify you. You tell me that you anticipate me causing you harm or killing you. Then, later, you come out into the freezing cold without even a cloak to keep yourself warm just to be with me. I don't know what to do."

"I don't want you to do anything," I say. "I understand why you wanted my father to pay for his crimes. It's your decision when my time has been served."

His face twists. "That does nothing to help me, my beauty. If I had it my way, you wouldn't want to leave. You wouldn't want me to release you."

"You don't even know me, Beast."

"I know enough."

"Like what?" I stare up at him, watching as snowflakes melt against his wet black nose, waiting for some kind of answer.

"I know that you're kind. Selfless. Brave. Fierce. You believe strongly in yourself and what's right. You've proven that many times. Usually, to my irritation."

I can't help but smile. "Mother always said I would be a danger to any man who wanted me as his wife. An eternal thorn in his side."

"What's a rose without her thorns?" he asks, tilting my chin up to face him.

"Defenseless," I whisper.

"And you, my beauty, are far from defenseless."

I don't want to look away. His compliments should mean nothing to me, sweet nothings from a man who has made his intentions clear. He wants to possess me on his terms, and he's only just recently considered what I want. Despite all of that logic, the praise he speaks makes my heart flutter, a humming-bird trapped beneath my ribcage. I don't want him to stop. I want to hear more, to know all the things he thinks about me.

"I needed you to protect me in the woods," I remind him.

"That was hardly a fair fight," he says gently. "Even I would have difficulty taking on a pack of wolves alone."

"You're just saying that."

"Why do you think I killed the one in charge?" he asks. "Had there been any other way, I would have let them all live, but they smelled blood. They were going to fight if I didn't make a monster of myself. In all the years I've been...like this, I've learned that those that see you as a wild animal will refrain from bothering you. They leave you be when they fear you. Most times."

"Most times?"

"Well, there are the villagers at the bottom of the hill. The ones who live in town. They know not to bother me. And then there's you. The woman who willingly broke into my castle. Who traded herself for her father. Who admitted her fear but refused to cower from it." He strokes my cheek softly, leaving warm heat in his fingertip's wake. "You may think I simply want to possess you, but the truth is, I long to understand you. I've never met a woman like you before."

"Maybe you have." I turn away, looking at the bushes of flowers that simply refuse to wither in the winter weather. "There are plenty of women in the world like me."

"Perhaps," he concedes. "But I have you here, and you're the only woman like you that I'm interested in learning more about." The smile on his face squeezes at my heart like he's reached a paw through my chest and done it himself.

"You're shivering, Isla. We should go inside." He rises from the ground, extending a hand to me. With his help, I stand up, brushing my dress free of any snow. I look back to see him staring at me, watching with amusement.

"What?" I ask, smiling shyly.

"Nothing. It's just...you. Come here for a moment," he says, pulling me toward him. He wraps his arms around me, and soon, the chill of the night disappears. He's like a warm blanket wearing a shirt and trousers, and I press my face to his chest, soaking up his heat.

I can hear his heart beating in his chest, much slower than any I've heard before. It's rhythmic, over and over, and I focus on it while I warm up.

"Isla," he says.

"Hm?"

"Thank you. No one has ever come out to talk to

me about my mother or father. Not that I've made myself all that approachable."

"You don't have to thank me."

He stares down into my eyes for a beat. "I do. Thank you."

"You're welcome, Beast," I say. Neither of us is willing to break eye contact first, and while I don't hear his speed up, I can feel my own heart pounding in my chest, especially when Beast lowers his head. My clouds of breath stop just as he kisses me.

At first, I expect it to feel strange, something nightmarish and uncomfortable, but he's gentle with me. Beast's lips are thin and soft, human in that regard, and when his tongue brushes against mine, I'm greeted with the most peculiar texture. It's larger than mine and warm, but that's where the similarities end. His tongue is firm, and against my own, I can feel the depth that each valley has.

It shouldn't make me stir beneath my skirt, but unlike Beast, I'm only human. I can't resist the wretched thoughts that race through my mind, of all the places and ways I'd like to feel his tongue. His body heat warms me to my core, as if defrosting something inside of me that's been frozen for years. Shocked by the inexplicable, animalistic urge, I step back, covering my mouth.

Beast looks at me with concern. "Did I hurt you?"

he asks, and to my surprise, he sounds genuine. He cares that he might have done something wrong.

"No," I say, shaking my head and willing my body to relax. "It's not that. It's just...new to me. That's all."

"I understand," he says with somber eyes. "You hate it."

"No!"

But before I can make my argument, he turns and marches back to the castle, his large cloak dragging a path through the snow. Guilt weighs me down, nearly enough to cause me to sink into the ground. It's not that I hated it that upsets me.

It's that I enjoyed it.

7

Ever since the kiss, I've had a week of
sleepless nights. A week of lying in bed,
eyes glued to the ceiling as I try and force
myself to sleep. Nothing seems to work, and Beast is
beginning to realize something is wrong. Yesterday at
breakfast, he asked if I was having trouble sleeping
because of the bags beneath my eyes.

I don't know why I lied and said that I was
sleeping fine. Maybe because I don't want to give him
another reason to dote on me. After our kiss, he's
been different. Less aggressive, always attentive to
everything I have to say. Not that I mind. I much
prefer this version of my host over the one that
throws tables and threatens me.

He now cares enough that if I were to complain
about my sleep, he'd do something about it.

He said that he didn't understand me, but I'm the one who's left confused. One moment, he's rejected himself before I could, putting words in my mouth, and then the next, he's trying to accommodate me and make me feel better. I know that he would move mountains if I told him I didn't like the way they looked.

That's why I can't talk to him about this. This issue with sleep is something I must deal with on my own.

After dinner a few hours ago, I snuck off to Mrs. Potter's room to take care of the problem myself. When I explained what I was having trouble with, she recommended I use a recipe of hers. She learned it from a sorceress years ago. A special tea for falling asleep on particularly rough nights. After memorizing all the ingredients, I hurried through the halls of Highburn back to my room, waiting until it grew late before I slipped from my room once more.

The castle seems even quieter at night. It feels like I'm in my own world, padding down the stairs and cursing myself for not stopping to grab my slippers. The chilly stones are almost too cold to handle on my bare feet.

In the kitchen, I start a small fire and use one of the many pots to begin the tea. I repeat the recipe over and over again, making sure I have every ingredient. While it simmers from the heat of the flames, I warm my hands over the fire.

A sudden noise behind me makes my heart leap, and I spin around to find Beast's hulking silhouette framed in the door. He wears only a pair of trousers tied at the front, and even in the darkness, I can see the broadness of his chest and the dark nipples barely visible beneath his fur. He steps into the light of the kitchen candles, giving more visibility to his body.

Immediately, I'm taken back to the night he pulled me to his body and kissed me. The way his large tongue brushed against mine with surprising tenderness was enough to leave me melting then, and from just the thought alone, even now.

"What are you doing?" he asks.

I expect him to be mad at me for leaving my room so late, but he only seems curious. "I...felt restless. Mrs. Potter gave me a recipe for this tea. I thought I might try it to help."

"Trouble sleeping?"

"Yes, but it's nothing to worry about," I assure him, forcing a smile when all I want to do is yawn restlessly. I'm craving a good night's sleep, and I'm more than willing to receive it. It just won't happen.

I put a momentary pause to the conversation when I stop to pour myself a mug of the amber liquid. I spoon a few heaps of sugar in, just as Mrs.

Potter said. According to her, the tea is as bitter as dirt without lots of sugar to help soften the blow.

When I turn, I find Beast still eyeing me. "Is your room uncomfortable? I can have it adjusted for you if that would make it easier."

"No, it's not that." I stir the tea slowly, watching the dark water ripple and move. "Ever since I was a girl, I haven't liked to be in the dark. It doesn't bother me most nights, but lately... I don't know. I can't sleep, and sitting in that dark room alone, just makes me anxious. Afraid."

Beast nods slowly, resting a hand on the table between us. "Would you like to come to my room?"

"What?" My gaze snaps up to his, shocked to hear such a question.

"I don't want you to be afraid here, Isla," he says. "It might make you more comfortable to have someone else there with you."

The worst part is that he's right. When I was a girl, and my fears became too great, Elyse would crawl into bed with me, and almost immediately, that unease would settle. I focused on her breathing, the way her chest rose and fell rhythmically, and in no time at all, soon we were both asleep.

But this is different. This isn't my sister. This is Beast, the one keeping me here in this castle with him against my will. The one who kissed me in the garden days ago. The one I didn't fight off.

"I couldn't," I say. I know that it's not a good idea. Being that close to him after what happened in the garden... This seems like a recipe for trouble, and the only thing I'm halfway decent at cooking is this tea. Yet there's a twist in the pit of my stomach at the thought of being close to him again. It's sick, but it's true.

It's an allure that I've never felt before. At least, not this intensely. He's dangerous. Bad news coated in thick gray fur. Yet I can't seem to stop the twisting knot in my stomach from clenching tighter as he steps closer. The heat radiating off of him rivals the fire.

"If you're afraid, you shouldn't sleep alone," he says, hardened eyes showing no signs of budging.

"I'm okay," I insist.

"Isla."

"Beast."

Sighing from his nose, Beast rounds the table and picks me up from the ground, grabbing the tea with his other hand. "I'm fine!" I insist, but he ignores my protests. He hefts me over his shoulder, and though I want to argue, I also feel a smile forming.

"Beast," I whine, trying halfheartedly to escape his hold. "Put me down."

"Not yet."

He carries me up the stairs and through the halls until he pushes open the door to his bedroom with his foot. A moment later, he tosses me onto the bed with little effort. I huff and sit up, ready to snap at him. Instead, I pause, taking in his room. It's only a bit larger than my own, but it's far more extravagant.

The left wall is lined with bookshelves filled with dusty tomes, and beside that is a comfortable chair to read in. A large fur rug is spread out near the crackling hearth, and oddest of all, a large golden wood piano rests in the corner of the room. I've never heard him play before. I wonder if he even knows how.

"You will sleep here tonight," he says, placing my tea on the table beside the bed. "Just for tonight. You have nothing to be afraid of."

Instincts nearly drive me to remind him that he himself is a monster, but I bite my tongue and nod at him as he rounds the bed and lies down on the left side. "Thank you," I murmur, watching as he undoes the knot at his pants. My heartbeat quickens, eyes flicking to the fire, then back at him, embarrassed at his lack of shame.

I nearly choke on my tea when I see that there's nothing between his legs. Amusement decorates his face, and he chuckles before he lies down beside me.

"It's impolite to stare, my beauty."

"I..." I don't know what to say. "I'm sorry. I just didn't... I don't know."

"I have a cock," he says simply. I hate the way it reassures me. Not because I'm particularly interested in that part of him, but knowing that it's somewhere reminds me once more that he's still somewhat human. Although...

"What does it look like?"

He raises one eyebrow up at me. "Would you like me to show you?"

"No," I say quickly, humiliation burning my cheeks. "I shouldn't have asked."

"What you mean is, is it human, or does it look like an animal's prick?"

I flatten my lips together and nod slowly, looking over bashfully at him. An anatomy lesson from a beast is not the way I predicted this evening would go.

"It's nothing you have not seen before. No spikes. No knots."

"Oh." Relief settles over me.

"It's just much larger than any man's."

"Oh." Mortification settles over me.

"Enough about me. You should get some sleep." He nudges the mug of tea in my hands toward me, and I take another sip, staring back at him.

The flavor is bitter, just as Mrs. Potter warned, but beneath it, there's a kind of sweetness that complements it. It makes the tea all the more palatable and helps the drink go down easier. Beast doesn't once break eye contact, his lids growing heavier the longer he watches me. When I finish the drink, I set it aside, already feeling a bit sleepy.

"How was it?" he asks.

"Not the worst thing I've ever had. I think it's working."

"Good. Now, sleep."

He lifts the blanket on my side of the bed and allows me to slide underneath. Once I'm comfortable, he crosses the room and extinguishes the fire. For a moment, the fear begins creeping its way back up my spine, but I remind myself that I'm safe. Beside Beast, I might be safer than I ever was before. If a pack of wolves couldn't get to me, the nightmares and anxiety are no match.

In the darkness, beside him, I say, "Thank you, Beast."

"Of course." It's a short grunt of a response, but I'm glad that I've thanked him. Since we've talked, he's changed his behavior. He's still frightening when I see his irritation nearly breaking free, but no tables have been flipped, and no dishes have been shattered.

I settle down next to him, my back to his front,

and close my eyes. I feel myself growing heavier, sinking into a dream, when I jerk awake, heart beating almost painfully fast. It's as if consciousness is fighting me, refusing to let me push it down into submission. I let out a groan of frustration.

"It's okay. You'll get there," Beast says, sliding closer toward me. Hesitantly, he drapes his arm around me. It's like a heavy, furry weighted pillow on my waist, but it's nice. A reminder that I'm not alone in this endless space void of light.

"I didn't hate the kiss," I whisper. I know that he can hear me because his hand twitches against my hip.

"You don't have to lie."

"I'm not lying. I liked it. And that scared me."

"Why?"

I bite my bottom lip. "Because no one's ever made me feel like that. No man has scared me and intrigued me like you. You're...you're both wild and proper. Volatile but occasionally gentle. And you make me feel safe. Safe and...and desired."

"You are desired, Isla. So incredibly desired."

When I shift again, his hand falls to my lower thigh, warm fingers brushing against my bare skin. I know I should readjust, try to maintain some sort of modesty, but all I can think about is our kiss in the garden. How small but protected I felt. From the harsh chill of the snow, and from whatever else roamed those woods looking for prey.

Just as much as he can be dangerous, Beast has a way of making me feel incredibly fortified. It's a confusion I've never faced, two opposing sentiments trying to cohabitate in one space. Logic versus emotion—and emotion just might be winning out.

His hand feels foreign on my body, but not something I turn from. When he slides his hand higher, just beneath my nightgown, I let out a soft breath between my teeth, ashamed of the way goosebumps spread across my skin in the wake of his trailing fingers.

He presses closer to me, his body flush with my back, and he lowers his head to mine, inhaling deeply. "You smell sweet," he murmurs in that voice that only seems more dangerous in the darkness of his room.

"Thank you," is all I can manage to get out.

"I wonder," he continues, his hand inching higher, pushing my gown past my hips. "Does my beauty taste just as sweet?"

God, I don't want to, but my body responds against my will. Wet heat grows between my legs, and I shudder beneath his touch. It's as if somehow he can control me better than I can. Instincts scream to run. Shove his hand aside and hurry back to my own bed. But I'm paralyzed, trapped between his large frame and his large paw stroking my skin.

"Are you going to let me taste you, Isla?" he purrs, dragging his nose over the curve of my ear. "I can smell how excited you are."

Embarrassed, I clamp my legs around his hand. "I..."

"I won't hurt you," he murmurs, his breath hot on the back of my neck. "Not unless you ask me to." I squirm against him, overwhelmed by all of this.

Finally, I relax again, parting my legs and allowing Beast access. A deep, rumbling laugh escapes him. It only makes me grow wetter, dampening the thin pair of underwear I have on. Not that that's much concern, because a moment later, I feel him drag a claw down my hip, tugging down the fabric until I'm left naked from the waist.

The pad of his finger strokes over my clit, and I gasp. It's unlike anything I've ever felt, somehow rough and tender at the same time. It could easily be an unpleasant experience, but he knows the right force to use. The right amount of pressure to add to make my knees shake and my stomach clench.

He works his finger in slow circles, and I'm torn between two thoughts. The first; that this is so wrong. That it defies nature. This was never meant to happen, this unholy experience. The second; that no other man has ever drawn this out of me. Left me turning beneath his touch, soaking and unable to put cohesive sentences together.

"Give me permission, Isla. Choose to be mine," he says. His tone is coy—like he's taking pleasure in throwing my words back at me. Instinctively, I want to push him away and not give him the satisfaction, but satisfaction is at the forefront of my mind, and I can only nod slowly in response.

"No," he growls, lips pressed to my ear. "I want to hear you say it. Out loud."

I swallow down a dry throat, eyes clenched tight, as he works my clit, in even more intense circles. When I take too long to reply, he swats it, sending a shock of lightning through me. I cry out, starting to curl in on myself. Beast is faster, though, and he slips his free hand around my throat, unfurling me.

"Be mine," he whispers. I feel his warm tongue trace the shape of my ear, and I come undone entirely.

"I'm yours," I say through shuddering breaths. "I'm yours, Beast. God, I'm yours."

Soaking in the pleasure, he laughs darkly in my ear before I don't feel him anymore. Not against me, not his hand around my throat nor his fingers on my body. I let out a groan and open my eyes to find him moving to the foot of the bed.

In the moonlight, he practically glows, his silver fur ghostly and his eyes hazy with lust. I feel my heart quicken as he drags his hands over my thighs, parting them to reveal my pussy. And then there's the purr again, the pleased rumbling in his chest that he has no control over. I make a similar noise as I watch him lower himself, closer and closer.

I expect him to pounce, to ravish me the way a monster might, but he's torturously slow instead, running his claws lightly up my inner thighs as he spreads me open. His bright eyes flicker up toward mine, and I swear that I can see him give a human-like smirk. He's too aware of what he's done to me, the vulnerability I've shown him, and he's relishing in it.

Even more cruelly, when he finally leans in to lick me, he stops just short of where I want him most. He traces the rim, prolonging pleasure for his own sadistic satisfaction. It's not until I let out a breathy plea that he complies.

"Please, Beast," I say, shivering. "I need it. I need you."

The relief that washes over me when he finally, graciously gives me what I need hits me right in the stomach. My head falls back, and I release the deep moan I've been just on the brink of expelling. His tongue traces my lips carefully, both sides, before he presses the flat of his tongue against my pussy and licks over it.

Beast peppers kisses over me, intercutting them with strokes of his tongue, and I can barely sit still. I force myself up on my elbows, trying to regain a bit of control through watching him. He doesn't mind the audience. When his eyes meet mine, I see them darken. He pushes one large finger inside of me at the same time he turns his attention to my clit.

His flicking tongue is repetitive, building a rhythm with his finger as he curls it and begins to work it in and out.

"Yes," I whisper. My abdomen clenches, and I put my feet flat on the bed, giving me leverage to push back against him. Watching his smile spread before he begins kissing my clit again only makes me wetter. It's been so long since I've had this kind of experience. I can't recall the last time a man has even wanted to do this.

But here Beast is, enjoying it as much as I am, fingering and licking and kissing me like it's the most important thing in the world. The appeal of it overrides any other reservations I've held since arriving in Highburn Hold. None of that matters, not when I have this monster of a man lapping at my pussy like it's the sweetest thing he's ever tasted.

Beast adds a second finger this time, and I feel

the sting of the stretch. It offsets the pleasure in the most delicious way, and I can't help but bring a hand to my breast, tweaking my nipple over the silk nightgown. My hips move with a mind of their own, rocking forward to meet each stroke of his fingers, taking him to the base of them.

"That's a good girl," he murmurs, pressing wet kisses against me. "Fuck yourself on my fingers, my beauty. Does that feel good?"

"Yes," I groan, my hips snapping forward for emphasis.

"How good?" Beast curls his fingers inside of me, stroking my walls in a way that knocks the breath from my lungs. God, I want to cry. I want to scream, to lose my mind beneath his touch. To let out a side of me that I've never seen, one I don't even know all that well.

"So fucking good," I force through a tight throat.

"Mm, if only you had listened to me—"

Before the last words can escape him, I reach for his horns, pulling his lips to my pussy to shut him up. He chuckles deeply before he returns in full force, kissing and sucking on my clit, dragging his hot tongue over my lips and nipping at my inner thighs.

Somehow, it's even better than before now that he's more enthusiastic. He even shocks me with a bite to the inner thigh that he soothes with slow, languid strokes of his tongue. All of it, from the way he massages my skin to the way he stares up at me to see how he's doing, it ruins my resolve completely.

I feel the warmth between my legs grow, to consume all of me, my whole body alight with this feeling of euphoria that's wholly unique to me. No other man has touched me like this. Beast is my unbecoming, and I come hard enough to cry out audibly, back arched, head back, rolling my hips against his face.

He greedily cleans me, making sure not to waste a drop. And when I collapse onto his sheets, trembling from the weapon he calls a tongue, he climbs my body, kissing his way up until he reaches my mouth. I can barely muster the strength to open my eyes to stare at him. When I do, I find that hard golden gaze softening.

Without thinking, I kiss Beast. I thread my fingers through his mane and kiss him, all too willing to taste myself on his thick tongue. He pulls back, and I pull him closer, refusing to let him go.

"It's your turn," I tell him. I want to reciprocate after the way he's just made me feel.

"No," he says lightly, dragging a claw along my cheek. "We'll have plenty of time for that. For now, you sleep."

"But—"

He traps my protest between our lips in another kiss. "Sleep, my beauty."

Though I want to argue, to show him the same kind of pleasure he's shown me, the allure of sleep has only been multiplied. Beast slides off of me, returning to his side of the bed. He pulls me close to him, one arm over my waist like before.

"Sleep," he encourages, and within minutes, I lose yet another battle, only this time, I'm happy to admit defeat.

8

To say that Beast enjoys spending time between my legs is an understatement of colossal proportions. He doesn't simply enjoy it. He thrives there. In the past three weeks, I've lost count of how often he's tucked me into bed after he's made me come a minimum of three times. And he doesn't want more. He doesn't demand that I reciprocate, and every time that I've offered, he's turned me down. Said that we'll get there eventually. For now, on my back and spread open for him is the only thing he needs from me.

"Isla?"

Mrs. Potter's voice snaps me out of the memories of this morning, particularly when Beast let me climb on top. I blush and look up at her, smiling. "Hm?"

"Did you hear me? You seemed somewhere else."

"Sorry, I just..." But there are no excuses I can come up with. Gratefully, Mrs. Potter doesn't seem to care because she reiterates the point that I missed in my daydream.

"I asked if you wanted to join me and Charlie in the kitchen today. He's been asking about you so much since he learned that you were staying in the castle."

All the filthy thoughts in my mind are cast aside instantly. "Has he really?"

"Oh, yes," she says, laying undergarments to fold them and store them in my armoire. "We're actually baking a cake today, so if you'd like to be there, I'm sure he'd love to meet you."

"Of course!"

It goes without saying. Being held in this castle for so long, I've forgotten how nice simple things like children and animals can be. I've seen birds and deer from my window, but oddly enough, no wandering children around. Knowing that Charlie's around excites me, so I agree without a second thought.

He doesn't disappoint, either. He's only about ten years old, but he's smarter than most men I've met in my life. He has curly blond hair, a dimple in both cheeks, and a playfully impish look in his eye that all boys his age always seem to possess.

He's inquisitive, too, asking all kinds of questions

about my life before I came to the castle. He informs me that his mother died during childbirth and that Mrs. Potter has been raising him since he was a baby. She's more of a mother to him than a grandmother, a role that I'm sure would take a toll on any woman her age. Still, it makes me respect her even more than I already do. She's a kind woman, selfless in ways that I can only aspire to be.

As we mix the cake in a large bowl, Charlie sneaks a bit of a taste with his finger, giggling when Mrs. Potter swats at him.

"How come you're spending so much time at Highburn, Miss Isla?" Charlie asks.

Mrs. Potter glances at me, then says, "She's a friend of Mister Lovell's."

"But he doesn't have any friends."

Mrs. Potter shoots him a warning glare. "What have I told you about saying that?"

Charlie drops his head so that it hangs against his chest. "Sorry, Grandma."

I simply smile, doing my best not to get involved with this. The last thing I want is Mrs. Potter getting stern with me too.

The knock at the door cuts our conversation short, thankfully. Mrs. Potter dries her hands off on a rag and says, "I'll get that. You two stay here."

"Okay, Grandma!" Charlie says. On her way out

the door, she pauses to kiss the top of the boy's blond hair.

"So. How come you're really here?" Charlie asks me when his grandmother is out of earshot. His cherubic face turns mischievous, bright eyes narrowing in the most adorably suspicious way. It's because of that look that I can't keep up the lie.

"Well," I say, mixing the cake mix slowly and racking my brain. "I made a deal with Mister Lovell."

"What kind of deal?"

"My father got into some trouble with him, and I decided that since he wasn't feeling so well, I'd spend time here with Mister Lovell instead. I keep him company. He's very lonely, you know?"

Charlie scrunches up his face. "He's mean. I hear him yell a lot. Well, not as much anymore. Not since you got here."

I can't help but smile at his reply. "I had to talk to him and tell him not to yell inside."

"Really? You told Mister Lovell what to do?"

"I sure did," I smirk. "Told him that he can't be a big mean monster to everyone in his life, especially not to me. And he's trying to be better now."

"Wow," is all Charlie says, awestruck by the idea of me telling Beast how to behave. In his defense, it's almost hard to imagine, but it's the truth. He may be bigger than everyone else here, but that's no excuse for his behavior. It's nice to hear that he's turned it around.

"I like you, Isla," Charlie says simply, scooting closer on the counter. He smiles wide, and I can see a chipped tooth in his mouth.

"What happened there?" I ask, gesturing to his teeth.

"Oh, that," he says, fiddling with his thumbs. "Grandma told me not to play in the woods, and I didn't listen. I fell over and broke my tooth a little. She was mad when she saw it."

"I bet," I chuckle. "If you ask me, it looks kind of neat."

His eyes light up excitedly. "Really?"

"Really!"

Mrs. Potter returns to the kitchen with a peculiar look on her face. She pulls me aside, and in a low voice, says, "Your sister is at the door. She says she needs to speak with you. It's urgent."

My heart stops.

Elyse? Here, at Highburn Hold?

Without another word, I give Mrs. Potter a nod and remove my apron, hurrying out to the door. I find her waiting with her arms crossed, her hair pulled into a sloppy braid, and her dress all wrinkled from the horse ride here. She doesn't look that well, and that only makes me more concerned. Elyse looks up at the sound of my footsteps and, without warning, throws herself into my arms.

God, it feels good to hold her again. I'd grown used to the idea that I would never see my sister again. Beast has said that he wants me to stay for good, and while I love Elyse dearly, I simply can't break our agreement.

All of those concerns fade the moment I have Elyse's body against mine. She seems so much more frail—like I might break her in half if I hug too hard. It kills me to see her this way when I've been living with Beast and baking cakes with Mrs. Potter and Charlie. I pull back to get a good look at her, fighting the urge to tear up.

Her skin is pallid, almost lifeless, and the bags beneath her eyes have grown even more sunken. She's worse for the wear. She's aged since I've last seen her, and it breaks my heart into the smallest of fragments.

"What's wrong, Elyse?" I ask, finally finding the strength to pull myself from her arms. For a long while, she can only cry, her tiny body trembling in my arms. I wipe the tears from her face and cup her cheeks, desperate to soothe her heartache. "Elyse, what is it? Why did you come here?"

"It's Father," she says through quaking breaths.

"Is he...?" I can't even form the words. He can't be. It's too horrible.

"No," she says. "But he's not got much longer. I had the physician from East Graybrook come in to see him. He says it could happen any day now. I've talked to him, and Father says he's ready to go, but not until he sees you one more time."

Now it's my turn to cry. To think, I've been living so carelessly, so frivolously, while my sister and father have been struggling. I can't stomach the thought of all the moments of happiness I've had in the past few weeks. Not when images of Father clinging to life because he wants to see me one last time appear in my mind.

Elyse hugs me once more, rubbing her hands up and down my back. "You have to come see him, Isla. Please. That's all he wants. Then he can move on."

Guilt practically drags me down to my knees. There's no way that I can leave. Not when things have finally started working for Beast and me. Not when I've spent every night in his bed since the evening I made Mrs. Potter's special tea. Beast has grown accustomed to having me beside him. There's nothing I could say that would convince him to allow me to leave.

"She will leave with you tonight."

I turn to find Beast standing atop the staircase, eyes focused on me and Elyse. He looks somber but confident in his decision. It's a matter of fact to him.

When Elyse sees him, she gives a start, her hand over her heart. In any other moment, it might be entertaining to see her reaction to Beast's appearance.

"Are you sure?" I ask him hesitantly. I don't want him to be mad at me. I don't think I'm strong enough to deal with another fit of his rage on top of the knowledge of my father's health.

"Positive. You can take my horse into town tonight. Stay with him until he's passed. And after that, you'll return here. Is that understood?"

This is more than I could've asked for. I don't know why he's letting me leave, but I suspect it might have something to do with his mother. Perhaps he's recalling the time he spent with her during her sickness. Perhaps he's just feeling generous. Either way, I can't ask questions. I won't let him have time to change his mind.

"It's understood. Thank you."

"I... I..." Elyse is at a loss for words, still gaping up at Beast long after he leaves us to our conversation. "Was that him?"

"Yes. I know." She has to be going through a range of emotions to process this, and under other circumstances, I might try to help her. Right now, however, all I can think about is Father. "We have to get home tonight, Elyse."

"Yes. We should leave as soon as possible."

"I'll pack right now."

"I'll help."

I take Elyse's hand in mine and give her a comforting squeeze. It's been so long since I've seen her that I want to hold onto her, never going another moment without her presence. As much as I crave that kind of connection, we don't have much time. Father could pass at any moment, and I need to be there with him.

Up in my room, I pack a sack full of clothing and underwear that I'll need for the trip. I have some of my clothes back home, but I want to be sure that I have enough. As I stuff my bag full, Elyse eyes me sadly.

"It's all so beautiful," she whispers. The longing in her voice cuts at me like a thousand tiny blades. It's not jealousy or envy of the possessions I have here at Highburn. It's sadness. Despair. Resignation to the fact that none of this will be hers.

"If there's something you see that you want, please take it. I have more than I could ever need."

"Really?"

"I insist," I say, gesturing to the wardrobe full of clothing. Dresses made of the finest silk and jewelry on the table beside my bed. It all means nothing to me. Not when Elyse is here with me again. I would trade it all in an instant.

"I couldn't."

"You can. And you will." I cross the room and grab a pearl necklace, holding it close to my heart. Beast delivered this to me two weeks ago, and while I agree that it's stunning, it means little when compared to how happy it would make Elyse. I hand it over to her, and she reluctantly holds it close to inspect it.

"It's yours now," I say, hugging her. "If you want to keep it, or sell it, or throw it away, that's your decision. Just...don't tell Beast that I gave it away."

Despite our situation, she smiles at me. "I won't."

When she puts it on, she looks gorgeous. It clashes with the ragged cloak and shirt she wears, but that only makes it stand out even more. "It's perfect on you," I say proudly.

"Thank you, Isla."

"No. Thank you for coming to get me. Now, we should get going. It's going to be dark soon, and I don't want to be out there alone when the wolves come out again." Beast might have been all the protection I needed back then, but even me and Elyse combined would still have problems.

"You're right," she says, walking to the door. I follow her, glancing back at my bedroom. Strangely enough, I'm going to miss having this little space. What was once a prison now feels like a room I can't wait to return to. Funny how Beast has been able to warp my opinions on things like that. He's full of surprises, namely allowing me and Elyse to go home.

When I return, I'll have to find a way to thank him for his kindness.

When.

Not *if*.

There's no question about that. I know it, and he knows it. That's why he's letting me leave. Beast knows that I will return. He's won. Rather than mulling over that reality, I follow Elyse downstairs, preparing myself for the ride back home.

✤ 9 ✤

I find a skeleton in Father's bed when we arrive home. In the few short weeks since I've been at Highburn Hold, Father has withered away, now just bones held together beneath thin skin and muscle. I want to reach forward and pull him into my arms, but I genuinely fear that the act might cause him pain. Instead, I collapse to my knees beside his bed, threading my fingers through his.

"Papa," I whisper, rousing him from his sleep. He blinks, dazed for a moment. When his warm brown eyes meet mine, it takes a moment for recognition to set in.

"Isla? My Isla?"

"I'm here, Papa."

He struggles to smile, and though the situation is morbid, and the finality of his life waits in every corner and crevice of our home, I've never felt happier. I made it in time to see him. He's not gone yet. I tighten my hold on his hand, using my other to run through his gray hair.

"I love you," he croaks. "I love you so much. Both of you. More than I've ever loved anyone else before."

It's almost cruel, hearing this as the seconds of his life pass away, but I let him speak. I let him tell stories of how we were always so self-sufficient, how we always took care of each other, and for a long time, didn't need him looking after us. The way he speaks is sadness covered in honey, sweetness dripping off every dreamy syllable. Father talks himself into a slumber, and when he's gone down to bed, I press a kiss to his forehead, tears streaming down my face.

I can only let them free when I'm in the safety of the bedroom, curling up into myself while Elyse rubs my back. It shouldn't be this way. I'm the eldest sister. I should be comforting her, telling her that the world will be colder, but we'll survive. Only I can't. Not today. Not now.

So, I let myself cry.

Sobs wrack through me until I'm left shivering beneath my blanket. Elyse is long gone, asleep in her own bed. I ache to reach out for her, but I remain where I am, allowing her to sleep. We'll both need our strength for when it's finally time.

That doesn't make the longing any easier.

My mind wanders to Beast.

Without a shadow of doubt, were he here with us, I'd be safe in his warm embrace, allowed to cling to him like a babe to its mother. His presence would be a comfort unlike it's been before. My throat squeezes tight, fighting the urge to call to him as if he would hear me. As if he would come running, bounding through the woods on all fours until he arrived at the door, out of breath and voice hoarse from such an exertion of energy.

The fantasy tugs at my lips until, for the faintest moment, I smile.

I WAKE TO THE SOUND OF ELYSE CRYING IN THE other room, and I know. I lie statue-still in bed, eyes squeezed tight, trying to focus my suddenly labored breathing.

He's gone.

I'm not sure what I expected to feel. Last night, I knew he wouldn't make it much longer, but I imagined I might have more time with him. More time to reminisce. To hear any stories of Mother that he might not have gotten to share with us before. To hold his hand one last time and feel his thin fingers trace over my knuckles as I stared down at him. I expected a lot.

But I only feel off-balance.

The room is spinning, and though I lie still, I feel myself swirling, spiraling toward the bottom of a pit that never seems to end.

I want to cry like Elyse. I know it would be cathartic. I know that it would probably soothe this fire burning in my throat to let the scream break free and reverberate throughout the room. It's easy to imagine the wail vibrating against the trees surrounding our home, echoing through the forest like the howl of distant wolves.

But I'm the strong one. I cannot fall apart when Elyse is already so broken. That's the one thought in my mind as I finally, against my better judgment, slide from beneath my sheets and step into the living room.

Elyse sits by the fire, nightgown crumpled beneath her, as she covers her round face. She appears so much younger, her grief taking her back two decades, not even four years old. When we were little girls, Elyse would cry just like this, curling in on herself, tiny whimpers escaping her suddenly, like hiccups. Whether it be a stomach ache or a skinned knee, she'd work herself up and fall to pieces over it, bleary-eyed and runny-nosed.

Just as I had then, I sit beside her and pull her into my arms. "I'm sorry," is the only thing I can think to say because I won't lie. We won't be okay for a long while. It will take even longer to manage the heartbreak. Part of me still hasn't recovered from Mother's passing, and now this...

I fight to contain it, but a single tear rolls down my cheek. Before Elyse has the chance to see it, I swipe my face and stare into the fire. I watch it crackle and dance, the flames licking bricks as it climbs the wall before receding. Impulsively, I want to put my hand in it.

Feel a different kind of pain.

A physical, immediate kind.

Anything other than the hollowness of loss. Adult orphans, that's what we are. Before, we had grounding, someone to keep us tied to the world. But now, he's gone, and this house, as well as my heart, feels vacant.

"I'm sorry," I say again, kissing the top of her head. "I'm sorry."

When the sun rises, Elyse has stopped crying. She stares blankly at the fireplace, the flames long since gone. Her cold cup of tea remains untouched, and her meal has gone to waste.

"Elyse," I say gently. "You have to eat."

"Not hungry."

I press my lips together and resist the urge to bother her again. I know she isn't hungry, but she looks gaunt as if worrying about Father has drained the life from her. She must eat. Something.

"I'm going to town to meet with the clergy," I tell her. "Will you manage without me for a few hours?"

"Yes," she hums, closing her eyes. "Please tell them to hurry. I can... I can already smell him."

I don't argue with her that this is impossible. He's been gone for hours, not days. Instead, I nod and lean in for a brief hug. I begin to pull away when Elyse clings to me.

"I love you, Isla," she whispers.

"I love you more."

The burial is quick. Painless. We say prayers for him, sending him off to eternal relaxation, but I can't bring myself to look into the eyes of the few mourners that have arrived. I just want to sleep. I just want to disappear, to not exist for a few days. Recover.

The hardest part is that soon, I must return to Highburn Hold and hand over my freedom once more. Though Beast has become more lenient with me, I'm still his captive, still his object. When this is all over, I'll have to leave Elyse here to recover while I lock myself back in that castle.

I worry about her.

During the burial, she kept her eyes closed in a fruitless attempt to contain her tears. They ran in crossing lines down her cheeks, and she filled the silence with soft moans of anguish. She's hurting so badly. I just hope that in my absence, she'll be able to find peace.

Father may not be with us anymore, but his pain is over. A kingdom of riches awaits him, and he will be rewarded for the endless sacrifices he made for us. I know that somewhere, out of sight, Father is happy and wishes he could tell us that.

When Father's buried and the last of the stragglers have left us alone, I take a seat in the kitchen and run my hands through my hair. It feels impossible that despite knowing this day would come, there's no way to truly prepare for it. I spent years trying to steel myself, from the moment Father first fell ill, and it was in vain. There's no way to ready yourself for this. No mantras to repeat that will defend you from the unstoppable truth that one day, the people you love will die.

God, I want it not to be so, but it simply is.

I turn to find Elyse sitting near the fireplace again. No more tears, but she seems distant. Will she make it without me? Will she manage the cruelty of the world without me by her side? I can't bear the thought of losing her to her grief.

"When are you returning to Highburn?" she asks softly.

"Tomorrow," I say. Tomorrow I must keep true to my word. Beast will be expecting me.

"I wish you could stay. That monster is... It's inhuman, what he's done to you."

I smile lightly. Humorlessly. "It is, but you've seen him. Human is no longer a word that applies."

"I don't know how you can stand to be around him. He gives me the chills."

"He's better."

"Better?" She turns to me, confused.

"We've made progress. Before, he was awful. Yelling. Throwing fits. But these days, he treats me better."

Elyse's eyes narrow, and she rises from her seat. "You like him."

"I do not."

I don't know how honest that statement is. I feel...something when I look at him. Maybe he's wormed his way into my heart. Or maybe it's the way his tongue feels against my inner thighs that has me confusing his lust with his affection. Whatever the cause, I don't hate him. I don't fantasize about killing him, or myself, to escape him. I must be unwell, I know.

It's why I don't think too long about this. About us.

"You're lying, Isla. You have a soft spot for him, do you not? He kidnapped Father!"

"I know this," I insist, too shrill for my own liking. "But he's never hurt me. Never forced me to do anything I don't want."

"How romantic," she says bitterly. I swallow back my own annoyance as she continues. "And what do you mean, anything you don't want? Have you..." Elyse's eyes are filled with horror.

"No." Another lie. "But he's not all beast. Or so, he tells me."

"You mean his prick?" she laughs. It's not an angry laugh. It's genuine amusement, something I haven't heard from my sister in months.

I can't fight off the smile. "That's what he said."

"I wonder what it looks like."

"I don't." At least, not often.

"It's probably the size of a man's leg," she murmurs.

"Watch your mouth!" I gasp.

"It's *your* mouth I'm worried about."

"Elyse!" But I can't help the fit of giggles that bubbles over. Soon, Elyse joins me, two immature adults laughing over Beast's anatomy like we're children again. It's a welcome change of scenery from the misery that's hung in the air lately.

"I wish you could stay longer," Elyse says so quietly that I barely hear her.

"I wish I could too. But I gave Beast my word."

"Why call him Beast when bastard is more fitting?"

I smile sadly. "One day you will meet him and see that he's far from the worst person in the world."

The way Elyse looks at me, hopelessness in her eyes, and her mouth curled downward, I can practically hear her thoughts. She thinks I've been brainwashed. That I've fallen for Satan himself. Were I in her position, I would feel the same. But I'm here because of his kindness. I was able to see Father one last time because of Beast. Despite all of his flaws—and there are many—I could never ignore this gift he's given me.

❧ 10 ❧

In the morning, the weather is miserable. Up above, the darkening clouds grow thicker, blocking out the sun, and casting an eerie, hollow white glow on the trees surrounding me. I urge Beast's steed Holly forward, convincing her to pick up the pace just a bit. Though there's nothing immediately threatening, I still feel a prickle of nerves on the back of my neck.

Holly trots forward, drawing us closer to Highburn Hold with every step. The feeling is a strange combination of relief and sorrow. To lie in Beast's arms and sleep without apprehension will be a luxury I wasn't aware I'd become accustomed to. But with the knowledge of my sister alone in our home, I don't know for certain that I'll be able to rest. To sleep peacefully, knowing that Elyse is truly, utterly alone.

I tighten my grip on the reins and straighten up my back. I can already feel the tension and stress from my thoughts, cramping up my shoulders and lower back. This trip is going to be a lot more painful if I don't loosen up.

When my stomach growls a while later, I slip from Holly's back and land down on my feet, a thick pillow of snow crunching beneath my boots. My breath escapes in tiny white clouds. From the satchel strapped to Holly's side, I pull a bit of bread and vegetables out, offering some to her. She sniffs at a carrot skeptically, and after a bit of soft-spoken coaxing, she eats one whole.

"Good girl," I laugh, running my hand through her mane.

Once I pull my hood over my head and tie up my cloak, I take a seat beneath an aged oak tree, biting into the bread and sighing. Because I had to leave so early in the morning, I didn't have a chance to properly enjoy breakfast. Though it may be a few days short of going sour, this bread very well might be the best I've had in months. The only thing that could make it better would be a spread of honey and spices to sweeten it.

I pop the last bit into my mouth and chew with satisfaction, eyes closed and head back against the wood of the tree. I'm so lost in the taste that I almost ignore the thought that pops into my mind, but it's insistent, demanding acknowledgment like a temper tantrum thrown by a child.

What if I left and never returned?

What if I turned Holly around, packed up the home, and ran away with Elyse? With Father gone, there would be no leverage. We could disappear into the night, and by sunrise tomorrow, we'd never be heard from again. Images of starting over begin to pepper my mind, at first falling like snowflakes and then growing into a flurry. Me and Elyse in a small cottage, weeks away from Graybrook, picking flowers and raising animals of our own. Freedom to move through this world as freely as we please. And sure, we might have trouble earning money, but before his death, Father taught us all of the life skills we'd need. Bargaining, pick-pocketing, and hunting. Elyse and I could manage it.

But what about Charlie and Mrs. Potter? Henry and Eve? The men and women who've made my time in the castle somewhat bearable. The ones most experienced and vulnerable to Beast's bouts of rage. I could never abandon them. I fear they might not survive were I to disappear entirely. I couldn't possibly give them a vision so hopeful as a version of Beast that doesn't abuse them, only to put myself first and run away. It would be cruel. A cruelty reserved for monsters.

It's a back and forth, these two images of Beast that seem to always find their way in front of me. The monster of a man so struck with anger that all rationality disappears from his mind, and the cursed loner desperate for company that he might truly care for. I want to hate him, to shun him just as Graybrook has, yet there's this part of me that wants to help, just as I did as a little girl when Father brought home wounded animals.

He told me that one day my heart would get me in trouble.

I didn't believe him then.

Frustrated, I rise and brush the snow from my skirts. Only then do I hear the approaching sound of hooves. I turn to find the source of noise just as two men come trotting down the road. The one in front glances at me impassively, but the one behind, without the thick beard or bushy eyebrows, can't take his eyes off me. He slows his steed to a halt a few feet away.

"Is everything well?" he asks, glancing between me and Holly.

"Yes, thank you," I say politely. "Just stopped for a bit of food."

"Shame," the younger blond says. "We could've

eaten together."

I press my lips into a thin smile and nod. "Shame." There's a long moment where neither of us say a word. I shift from foot to foot, unable to meet his eyes for very long. There's an animalistic urge inside of me to leave. Now. I say, "I should hurry back home," as I start for Holly.

"Where's home?" the older man asks, narrowing his eyes. "East Graybrook's that way." He jerks his thumb backward, the way I came from.

"Jacob is right," the younger one notes. "Only thing out that way is the woods."

Jacob's eyes never leave mine as he adds, "And that bastard's castle."

"Surely you wouldn't want to go that way. That's no place for a beauty such as you there."

My heartbeat quickens, that urge to flee growing from a faint whisper to a screech through the air. I grip onto the reins and say, "I really should go." Before I can mount Holly, I hear the crunch of feet landing on snow. There's a hand tangled in my cloak, pulling me away from Beast's horse.

"You're the one we've heard about, aren't you? The Highburn whore?"

His words are like a slap in the face, and I try to pull away from him hard. "Let go of me," I demand, jerking back to no avail.

"Answer the question, bitch. You live in Highburn Hold with that monster, do you not?"

"Wil, let her go," the older man sighs. He slides off the back of his horse and approaches us. When Wil's hands are free from my cloak, I stumble backward, pressed up against a tree. They convene at the same time, and up close, I can see that they favor each other. The same thin, pinched nose. Dark, bottomless brown eyes. Wil even has a bit of hair growing on his chin, though it's nothing to his older brother's beard.

"You can tell us the truth," Jacob says slowly, his eyes leering over me methodically. Taking in all of me.

"I—"

The words won't come. They hang in the back of my throat like icicles. I'm frozen in place, muscle tensed, eyes darting back and forth between these two strangers.

"It is her," Wil laughs cruelly. "Must be in a hurry to see that abomination again. Does he fuck you, whore? Do you let him mount you and have his way? Or does he even give you a choice?"

Anger roils inside of me, a rage born from utter terror over these circumstances. I shouldn't have stopped. I should have kept going, eaten on Holly's back. But the louder voice inside my head screams that I shouldn't have had to worry about these two. I deserve to eat where I want without being bothered. Insulted.

"There's the answer," Jacob muses, reaching forward to brush a strand of hair from my face.

"Don't fucking touch me," I snap, pulling away.

Wil's eyebrows rise, and he chuckles. "The whore's got a mouth on her."

"I'm sure that bastard puts it to good use." Jacob's hand is lightning fast, snatching me up by the chin and squeezing hard. "Perhaps we should have a taste of what that lucky fucker gets to enjoy every night."

"Perhaps we should."

Jacob's grip on my face tightens, and he yanks me forward, closer to the brothers. "Open that pretty mouth and show us what it looks like," he whispers. It's a terrifying noise, worse than the howling wolves from before. Shaking, I force myself to part my lips, eyes squeezed shut. Jacob makes a noise of approval and drags his thumb along my bottom lip. Slowly. Methodically. When he presses it inside of my mouth, I bite down until I taste blood.

All at once, an explosion. Jacob screams and rears back, and Wil's palm connects with my face hard enough for me to see stars. I stumble back, two, three steps until my heel catches on my skirt. The world tilts in the opposite direction, and my back connects with compacted snow with a hard thud. I'm spinning, tumbling backward, watching as Wil and Jacob grow smaller and smaller.

I don't stop bouncing until I connect with a tree at the base of the hill. Crackling pain shoots through my body, from my skull to my toes, and I'm left gasping for air, breathless. Everything is cold, numb. My fingertips. My toes. My blood.

In the distance, I hear the brothers shouting. With all my strength, I angle my head to the top of the hill, where the road is. I can see them both, Jacob clutching his bloodied finger while Wil points down at me.

I can't lie here. If I stay still, if I don't force myself up, they will find me. I don't know what they'll do to me, but I'm certain I'll wish I were dead. Against my body's protests, I plant my palms in the snow and force myself from the ground, crying out as my back fights my decision. But I have to. I have to.

When I look back to the hill, I see nothing. That's when I begin to run. Not to Holly, who must be terrified if she hasn't already fled, but in the opposite direction. Deeper into the woods. I'd rather see how I fare with the wolves than either of the brothers. Hiking my skirts and cloak up, I turn away from the road and run.

The winter air burns my throat raw, and though

all of my body begs for me to slow down, I refuse, pushing myself until I collapse down on my knees. I have just enough strength to hide behind the trunk of a large tree before I must stop.

The tears threaten to spill, but I hold them back, pressing my frozen fingers against my eyes to keep them from clouding my vision.

Not yet, I tell myself. *Not until you're safe.*

I've only started to regain my breath when I hear them. They're not close, but they're coming my way. My legs feel like hellfire, and I know that I can't rush again. Something like determination pulses through me, and I know that soon, they'll be on me. I'm prey to them, waiting to be slaughtered. They'll eventually find me if I don't do something.

My tracks.

When Father took us hunting during the winter, he told us to always be aware of the tracks animals left in the snow. The animals weren't smart enough to cover their tracks, and we managed to hunt down plenty of small game for dinner during those brutal nights.

I look back to see that the falling snow has hidden most of the footprints, but the ones beside the tree are still fresh. Any halfway decent hunter would see them and know where I went. I pull my cloak free and spread it out as far as it will go, patting the snow beneath flat.

"She must've gone this way."

Jacob's voice echoes through the trees, and my movements grow more frantic. I pack the snow as tight as I can, then ball up the cloak and toss it as hard as I'm able to manage in another direction. Perhaps they'll go that way instead.

"We should leave her, Jacob. Her horse is dead. She'll freeze out here soon enough."

"No," Jacob snarls. "I want to watch the life leave her eyes after I've had her. She nearly took my finger off, the cunt."

Visceral satisfaction burns deep in my chest. I wish I would've bitten harder.

"There's something up ahead."

Their footsteps are closer now, and my heartbeat quickens. Slowly, I reach beneath my skirts and remove my blade, squeezing it against my palm hard. It steels me. Steadies me. If they come this way, I'll be ready.

I risk a peek from behind the tree, pulling back when I see just how close they are. They stand only yards away, investigating the cloak.

Wil points to the left. "She's gone that way."

Jacob nods slowly but skeptically says, "Perhaps.

But she's smart. This could be a trick. You go that way; I'll keep going forward."

My stomach sinks, and I bite back a strangled, throaty noise of despair. It nearly worked.

"Good idea. Whoever finds her gets to have her first."

"Agreed," Jacob says, though there's a noticeable lack of enthusiasm in his voice. Something inside me says that if he finds me, I won't live long enough to fall victim to Wil.

I watch as the brothers break off, Wil heading further away as Jacob stands up straight and surveys the area. I press my back flat against the tree and try to steady my breath. Every exhale releases a white cloud of air, and he might see it.

"I know you're out here, bitch," Jacob says in a low voice. "You might have fooled Wil, but I know you didn't go that way. I'm going to find you, and when I do, I'm going to hurt you. Many times. Worse than that monster ever could."

A chill runs up my spine, and against every instinct, I don't take off running. Not even when the sounds of his crunching footsteps approach. Instead, I slide down the back of the tree slowly, clearing the snow.

"If you come out, maybe I'll be gentler."

His rumbling laugh threatens to freeze me in

place, but I continue to brush aside snow until I reach the dirt below. There, I begin clawing at it, nails scraping the surface. When the soft top layer is gone, and I've finally reach the hard, dry portion, I scoop out a handful, crumbling it in my fist to make it finer.

"I guess I won't be gentle, then."

Jacob's only a few feet away. Every hair on my body stands at full attention. I strain my ears for every step. Every movement. I hold my breath, stilling myself. Waiting. Waiting until I see movement to my left. My grip tightens around the blade.

"Found you."

I see the toe of his shoe pass by the tree, and I toss the dirt up into his face. "Fuck!" he screams, and before he can get out another word, I rise up and throw my full body into him, sending him stumbling backward. He swipes at his face, tears streaming down his reddened cheeks.

"Fuck you," I scream, lunging at him, blade aimed for the side of his neck. It presses through his flesh with startling ease. When I rip across, to the front of his throat and out, that's when I feel the resistance. Only just a little. Blood spurts from the jagged wound in powerful streams, squirting through his fingers when Jacob clamps a hand down on the wound.

He gurgles, wide eyes hollowed as his knees buckle. Jacob's movements are erratic, trembling spasms and twitches that rock him harder, harder, until he collapses, flat on his back. His hand falls from his neck, and all at once, he's dead.

My stomach churns, and the urge to vomit threatens to send me doubling over.

He's dead.

I watch as his throat continues to spit up blood, drenching the snow in vivid color. It's mesmerizing the way the red pools beneath him, spreading more and more until finally, the bleeding stops. He's really, truly dead because of me.

There's a part of me that wants to feel sorrow. I took a human life. I should feel something. Some kind of strike against my humanity, remorse, or regret for what I've done to one of His creations. But I feel nothing. The corpse is nauseating, but the action? The act of tearing into the throat of the man threatening to harm me?

That would have been me lying in the snow.

I'd rather it be him than me.

"You fucking bitch!"

The deep voice makes me jump, and I spin around just in time to see Wil barreling toward me. He tackles me to the snow, and we both hit the ground with a dull thud. In an instant, his hands are around my throat, tightening enough to cut off my breath.

"You killed him! You killed him, you goddamned cunt!" His eyes dart between me and Jacob's body. His body wracks with sobs, and the harder he cries, the more his fingers tighten. I thrash against him, panicked, frantic for a way to free myself. When I swipe at his face, he tilts his head back, avoiding my nails.

"I'm gonna kill you," he says through gritted teeth, hatred, unlike anything I've ever seen, burning in his eyes. Wil begins slamming my head down so hard I think for a moment that my skull will crack. The world grows fuzzy, darkening by the second. Desperately, I claw at the ground for my fallen knife.

"Die," he growls, hefting me from the ground by my neck, only to slam me down once more. Just as I'm lifted again, I find the handle of my dagger. In a weak attempt, I slash at his face. Wil howls in pain, letting me go so that he can cup his cheek.

Air rushes into my lungs so quickly that it hurts. I cough violently, rolling onto my side as the world becomes light again. I can just barely hear my own rattling gasps beneath Wil's wailing. I turn back to see him, horrified by the sight. A deep gash runs from the corner of his mouth up to his ear, and blood runs down his cheek like a waterfall. He tries to curse, but the words are lost in the gore, his spittle combining with the ichor that sprinkles the snow between us. He makes a lunge for me, crimson fingers outstretched, but I scramble backward, clutching my throat as the sting of strangulation sets in.

Wil is off-balance, and when he finds open air instead of me, he falls face-first beside Jacob.

The woods are silent as if every animal was made aware that predators would be coming. Uneasily, I push myself from the ground and wipe the tears from my eyes.

Not yet, I tell myself. *Not until you're safe.*

For a long moment, I do nothing but stare down at my attackers, their lifeless bodies outlined in red. I can only look for a moment at their corpses, the sight of the brothers grim. The chill of the afternoon air burns my face, and slowly, I force myself over to my cloak, pulling it on and tying it.

Though I'm far from the road, I'm certain I can make it back to Highburn before nightfall. It will take me longer without Holly, but I can do this. I pull my blade from the snow a few feet away from Wil and wipe the blood free, returning it to the sheath under my skirts. Then I begin walking.

I make it back to Highburn Hold well into the night.

❧ 11 ❧

When I drag myself up the steps of Highburn Hold, I can't feel my finger-tips. My whole body is frigid, frozen down to the marrow of my bones, and moving even one more foot feels like it might finish me off. A servant shining armor glances my way once, then twice, before she gasps and drops her rag by her feet.

"Miss Isla," she exclaims, running toward me with wide, fearful eyes. "What—what happened to you?"

She pauses to take in the sight, eyes traveling down from my disheveled hair to my blood-splattered gown, peeking through a frostbitten cloak. Her hand presses flat to my heart, and when she finally swallows hard enough to force words out, she says,

"We should get you by the fire."

I don't fight her as she drags me into the next

hall, sitting me down on an armchair and tossing more wood into the flames crackling beside me in the fireplace. Somehow, the fire feels even colder, the sudden warmth making me sting. But I don't pull away or flinch back the way my natural instincts instruct. I need this. Any longer in those woods, and I would have frozen to death. My fight would have been for nothing.

I can hear Beast before I can see him. The servant has only been gone for a moment before the heavy, impossibly powerful thudding of his footsteps ring through the first floor of the castle. He pushes the double doors open so fast that they crack against the stone walls. I jump, my heartbeat racing so loud I'm certain I can hear it.

"Where have you been?" he demands in that booming, terrifying growl. He bounds toward me like lightning, only, when he's close enough to see me in the light of the fire, he pauses, as if I've just startled him.

Beast's demeanor changes, snarl faltering, and brow bone softening into concern. "My beauty," he murmurs, dropping down to his knees to glimpse a better look of me. "What happened? Are you hurt?"

I stare into his eyes, two pools of warm honey gold that shine inconceivably bright. Those eyes are shadowed with doubt. With unease. My first thought is to quell his worry. Assure him that I'm okay. I survived. That means that I'm okay.

But it's a lie.

All of this is a lie.

These gorgeous dresses and his beautiful home. The way he looks at me. It all makes my stomach dance with butterflies, but it's all based on a lie. I did not choose to be in this castle. I did not choose any of these dresses. And the only reason he cares for me is because I am his. His kindness is dependent on my compliance. I can't do this anymore.

"You did this to me," I whisper through gritted teeth.

"I don't understand, my beau—"

"I'm not your *anything*." The words come out like broken glass, cutting my throat, spewed directly into his face. I rise to my feet, icy bones now thawed yet still aching. Still sore from the nightmarish journey through the woods.

"Be careful how you speak to me, my beauty."

"Or what?" I challenge. "You'll hurt me? You'll strike me down, the same way you strike down your servants? Leave me with scars and diminish my worth to you?"

Beast's eyes harden, but he remains silent. I'm not sure I want to know what thoughts race through his mind. What his animal instincts are telling him to do.

"Two men," I say, suddenly unable to breathe. The thought of their faces comes back to me so abruptly that I can't help but see them in both states. Predatory eyes gleaming as they approached me. Jacob's aimed skyward as his life slowly slipped away. The white of the snow. The red of their blood. The smell, thick and metallic, like pungent rust.

"Two men attacked me in the woods," I finally manage to whisper. I want to scream it in his face. "They knew where I was living. They knew I lived here. Said that since I was the beast's whore, they could do anything they wanted to me."

Every hair on Beast's massive frame stands in alertness. "Did they touch you, my—Isla? Tell me where they are. I will find them and rip their spines from their backs."

I smile sadly. "They tried. I put a blade in his neck. Pulled it from his throat and slashed open his brother's face. Mouth to ear. They're dead now. Holly's dead too."

It's Holly's death that brings tears to my eyes. In all of this, she was the most innocent. The one that deserved a safe return home. My throat clenches tight, and I feel my knees give out. Beast catches me in his arms before I can hit the floor, and I cling to him, sobbing.

This ache stings so differently. It's not the pain of losing Father, nor the heartache of leaving Elyse. This suffering throbs between my temples, a pounding in my head that makes me dizzy. I'm trapped here. Trapped in this castle with a monster, ripped from my dying father and helpless younger sister. Had I never come here, those two men's deaths wouldn't have been by my hands.

Beast says nothing. He holds me like I could break, with just the slightest bit of pressure, like I'm made of porcelain. A doll. That's all I'll be, in this castle with him. His beautiful, helpless doll.

"I wish you'd killed me that first night at supper," I whisper.

"I would never have killed you."

"Of course not," I laugh bitterly. I sniff hard and wipe my eyes, jerking back from him. "You would never dream of hurting your prized possession. That's what I am to you. Something for you to dress up, give gifts to, and lay down in your bed."

"That's not true, Isla," he insists, but I've had enough of his lies.

"But it is," I say, my voice rising. "I'm not a child, Beast. I know the way men like you think. You don't get upset that someone put their hands on me; you get upset that someone put their hands on what belongs to *you*. That's how you see me. Not as my own person, but as the prize you won when my father entered your home."

"Isla, do you want to leave?" His voice echoes off the walls of the castle. The outburst leaves me stunned, heart skipping a beat then quickly trying to catch up. "If you want to leave, I won't hold you any longer."

To prove his point, he crosses the room and opens the doors, steps through them, then opens the doors in the foyer. I follow him through the castle.

"You think so little of me, and I won't keep you here if you'd rather be free. You can walk through those doors now. I will send you home with another horse. Let you take all of the jewelry and dresses and valuables that you can fit in all your bags. If you want that, I will not stop you. I would rather watch you disappear into the blizzard and never come back for me than for you to even once think that I don't see you as someone independent of myself."

His eyes are wild again, but for the first time since I've been at Highburn, they're not filled with rage. That's all been replaced with something more urgent. Something more desperate.

"Never in my life have I been challenged the way you challenge me. The way you fight me is so frustrating, but it is *you*. Just as I'm not an easy man, you are not an easy woman. You make me wait. You make me *earn.* The prize is not to have you here in these halls with me but to have you smile at me every morning. The prize is that, for the first time in my life, you don't make me feel like a monster."

I swallow thickly down a raw throat, eyes brimmed with tears all over again. I can feel the eyes of servants on us, rendered just as silent as me. Are they struggling to believe that this is happening the same way I am?

"Isla, I will not beg you to stay with me. But what I will do is promise you that for the rest of my life, I will treat you the way you deserve. I will prove to you all the ways you've made me a better man."

It's not often that I'm left speechless. As a girl, I never hesitated to speak my mind, even when the consequences would be great. To not be honest with my words felt like a betrayal to myself. And yet, here I stand, unable to form a sentence to accurately express my thoughts. I want to hate him, this goddamned beast of a man. I was prepared to leave. Even if it meant not packing anything and walking home in the snowstorm once again, I would have gone.

But now he's so cruelly bared his underbelly to me. Shown me his weakness in front of the servants who, until this point, have only known him as some indestructible terror. It's the kind of sacrifice no man other than my Father has ever made for me. To be weak for the woman he cares for must eat away at him, and still, Beast stands in front of us all.

I wipe my eyes and take one step toward him, followed by the next, and the next. Soon, I must tilt my head back to look at him. His eyes soften the closer I move until his face is contorted into a hesitant grimace. He's practically holding his breath, waiting for an answer. Rather than saying a word, I run my fingers down the length of his shirt, stroking material that must have cost a fortune.

"I'm not going to leave," I say low enough for only the two of us to hear. His shoulders begin to relax, and to my surprise, he smiles. Nothing too big, but enough for me to catch it. That nagging feeling says to run, even still, but I've made my decision. I hate this man, and deep down, I think I might feel the exact opposite way as well.

"We should clean you up. You should get some rest, my beauty."

I don't bother arguing with him about this. I need to wash this blood off of me. I need to scrub the smell of death and sweat from my skin until I'm rubbed raw. When Beast takes my hand and guides me to the stairs, the servants quickly resume their duties, heads down, walking briskly.

A bath is drawn, and once I've slid into the hot,

bubbly water, Beast and I are alone in his washroom. His gaze lingers. I don't shy away. I scrub the dried and crusted gore from my hands and wrists, watching the red stains give way to pale, smooth skin below.

"Are you okay?" Beast asks me after a long period of silence. I pause, fingers lathering soap through my hair, and turn to him. From the tone of his voice, I know that he's not asking about what happened in the woods. He means Father.

"I'm...surviving."

"That's not what I asked, Isla."

"Then, no. I'm not okay."

The silence between us is heavy, and before it can press down on me and crush me entirely, I resume what I was doing, massaging the soap into my scalp. I start to lean back into the water when I feel the heat of Beast's paw on my back, keeping me up. His free hand is cupped as he dips it into the water, lifting it and pouring the water onto the back of my head. His touch is startlingly gentle, something I didn't know he was capable of.

"I'm sorry."

Two words that I'm certain are not commonplace around the halls of Highburn Hold. An admission of emotion. His apology feels like a gift.

"It's not your fault."

"I'm sure my reaction didn't improve his health,"

he murmurs, dragging long fingers through my hair. Without his claws drawn, they almost feel like the touch of a man. A man with impossibly large hands, of course.

"Maybe not," I reply. "But he was sick for a long time. Long before he ever met you. This was all inevitable."

It sounds callous, like my time in the woods froze my heart permanently, but I know that if I let the grief take me, I'll never have myself again. I'll lose that light, the one that keeps me moving forward, and for my sake and the sake of Elyse, I can't risk that. There's too much living left to give up.

"You should tell me about him."

"Maybe someday." I don't know if I ever will. He's come around quite a bit, but Beast still has his moments. Guttural reactions to how my father provided for us. Before, I could handle it, but things are different. That's a risk I'm not willing to take.

Beast's hands roam lower down my body, then back up again. He digs his fingers into my back, working the muscles that I've abused all day. It's the kind of painful relief that makes me moan—whether out of pleasure or pain, I'm not able to discern. The one thing I know is that I need this. I need to feel his touch, to know that with him beside me, I'm safe.

"You're incredible," he says, his voice right beside

my ear. I flinch, then just as quickly, release the tension, melting at his touch.

"What else?" I ask, eyes closed, head tilted back.

"You're strong. Smart. Resourceful. Caring."

His praises wash over me from the crown of my head down to my toes, and I groan louder than I expected. Were it not for the bathwater, I would surely feel myself growing wetter with every word of his acclaim.

I want him.

It's not a decision I consciously make. There's no moment of consideration, concern about what this means for me to be with him in this way. No hesitation, no toes dipping into water. It's a fact agreed upon without dissent. All in favor.

I need him.

I press my palms flat against the side of the tub, and without warning, I rise from the water. Soap runs down my body in a race to the bottom, and when I turn to face him, Beast's eyes are making that same journey. He looks up at me again, and it's like he knows. Like he can read my mind and understands that tonight, I don't just want what he's given me before—though I do plan on getting that as well.

I'm going to take him.

All of him.

Beast slips a hand around my waist and pulls me

flat to his chest. I soak through his white shirt the second we connect, but he's unaffected. "Can I?" he asks, voice husky. He's never sounded more attractive than he does in this moment.

"You can."

It takes no time at all for us to make it to his bed.

Beast sets me down on his bed and steps back, simply watching me. His eyes roam over me, and though I'm still a bit wet from my bath, I spread out on the bed in front of him. Spread my legs wider. Slip two fingers down to my stomach and between my lips. Beast lets out that approving purr when I press my fingertips inside my pussy.

"You're so beautiful," he breathes, his voice slightly ragged.

"So I've heard." A wry smile spreads across my face, and he mirrors it. I plunge my fingers inside suddenly, eliciting a quick, brief whimper from myself. "Don't make me wait any longer, Beast."

That must be the magic word because he quickly undoes the buttons on his tan tunic and slides it from his body. I always forget how much like a man he is, muscles rippling as he discards his shirt. The arms I've found comfort in at night now look almost threatening, and I can practically feel the power emanating from them. I want those arms. Around me. Pinning me down. Making me his.

Beast drops his pants and steps out of them, leaving him naked just like me. "Are you sure you're ready, my beauty?" he asks once more. I don't say a word. I only give him a slow nod, easing back onto the bed to watch him approach.

"Don't be afraid of it," he says, and I bite back the urge to roll my eyes. The number of men I've met who might say the very same thing.

But Beast isn't being dramatic or stroking his own ego. It's almost startling watching the tufts of fur between his legs part and a cock break through. I fight the urge to cover my mouth, but I can't look away as his erection rises from the hair. It keeps going, long past the point of stopping for any human male. Finally, he wraps his hand around it and gives himself a few tugs.

"The sorceress was mighty generous to you," I say, gaze flitting up to meet his.

He wears a smirk on his face, dark lips tugging up to one side. "The one area more of a blessing than a curse."

"I'd certainly say." I can't take my eyes off of him. I'm not sure what I was expecting, but it certainly wasn't something like this.

Beast's cock doesn't look spiked, or deformed, or misshapen. Nothing discolored or unsettling. He looks perfectly normal, like any other man of lighter complexion might have tucked away in his pants. Pale white flesh covers the shaft, and a pink tip caps him off. The difference is his size. I've never seen someone this large, thick veins racing from the head down to the base. I don't see any testicles either, which leads me to believe they're possibly internal.

I decide on that. Asking where they are seems a bit rude to me. Instead of asking, I slide forward on the bed and tentatively reach a hand forward to stroke him. Beast doesn't stop me. His eyes close briefly, and I add my second hand, his heat searing against my palms. He feels like human skin. Looks like human skin.

Somehow, it reassures me. I know that he's not some wild animal, but feeling it in my palms is a confirmation I didn't realize I needed until now. As I stroke him, a pearl of clear fluid beads at the tip, and I use that to add slickness to my movements. Beast rumbles out a groan, and I find myself smiling at him.

The mighty, powerful beast of Highburn Hold,

reduced to a moaning mass of fur and fangs and horns from something as simple as this.

When I take him into my mouth, it only pushes him further down that hole of desire, his hips stirring slightly to slide more past my lips. I recognize almost immediately that taking him all the way down will be impossible, but I swirl my tongue around as much as I can fit, humming satisfyingly when he places a large paw against the back of my head.

I bob forward and back, addicted to the taste of him, to the way he seems to scald my tongue and pulse against my lips. I desperately want to fit him all the way down, and I make up for what I can't reach with both hands wrapped around the base, stroking and squeezing him while I suck.

That groaning only grows louder, and when I look up, I find those golden eyes staring down at me in approval. He juts his hips forward in time with me, sliding his cock into my mouth just a bit further with every repetition. Not wanting to be showed up, I push past my limit, taking him further than I probably should, and groan hard when I have to pull back, coughing.

"Mm, slow, my beauty. We have plenty of time." He lowers himself for a kiss, his large tongue stroking mine with precise control. He wipes the prickle of tears from my eyes at the same time. When we break the kiss, he eases me back onto the bed.

"Are you ready?" he asks in a low hum.

"I am."

Flat on my back, he looks even larger, but I refuse to let my nerves get the better of me. I want this. The thought of it makes me damp, but seeing him up close like this has me soaked, far too eager for him. He climbs across the bed toward me, settling himself between my legs.

"Tell me when to go slow," he says, and I nod, watching as he takes hold of his cock and presses the tip against my opening. Just the stroke of him against me has chills running through my body and something stirring to life inside of me. A kind of monster I'm still afraid of. It wants more, wants every last bit of Beast inside. I don't fight it. In fact, I embrace whatever this yearning is, spreading my legs wider and inviting him inside. I let my head fall back and focus on breathing; readying myself for what I know won't be an easy experience.

It isn't.

He's almost too big to take, and I grip the sheets so hard my knuckles turn white. As if reading my mind, Beast slows his pace, easing into me and allowing me to stretch to fit him. He doesn't rush this, and I'm immediately grateful. I want it, I want to be full of him, but it's a delicate process. Patience is the only way to make this work.

I grow more comfortable with the feeling the more time we take, and a few moments later, I can feel our bodies connect fully. He's inside of me entirely, so full that there's no room for anything else. Not a perfect fit, but a painful, pleasant stretch that makes me want him even more.

"God," I whisper, a hand snaking down my body to touch my clit. I rub circles around it, massaging the bundle of pleasure that makes my toes curl and my stomach roil with intense churning. Beast simply watches, a predatory smile spreading across his face. Those teeth look even more intimidating in the candlelight. His bright eyes darken, and he places a hand on either side of my hips, holding me firmly as he begins to rear back and press forward. Each stroke of his cock inside me sends sudden bursts of ecstasy through me, and I groan loudly, head back against the bed, my fingers dancing against myself.

"Yes," I breathe, stifling a whine against my palm. "Yes, Beast, that feels so good."

He chuckles darkly and slides his hands down to the backs of my thighs. "If only you could see what I see," he murmurs in a low, rumbling voice. Beast pushes my legs back, eyes down as he watches himself disappear inside of me.

I want to see. I want to watch how easily he slides into me, how much he's filled me, but all I can focus on is the way his muscles ripple beneath the thin layer of short, white fur. He glows a ghostly bright color, and his broad chest heaves with effort as he thrusts forward repeatedly.

It takes time, but the sting disappears, and I'm on cloud nine, one hand between my leg and the other pinching at my nipple absently. To my surprise, Beast takes his time. He doesn't go faster or rougher than I can handle. This kind of control seems incongruous with the rest of him, but I must admit that tonight he's surprised me more times than I can count.

"Is that good?" he asks.

"So good," I breathe.

"Are you ready for more?"

It's such a simple question, but hesitation and excitement begin their own battle inside of me. I want more, desperately so. At the same time, am I ready for it?

"I am," I say. My voice sounds confident.

I've only just gotten accustomed to this new feeling when Beast lifts me from the bed, my whole world tilting. I collide with his chest and wrap my arms around his broad shoulders, clinging to him as he effortlessly lifts and drops me.

Each time sends another shockwave of pleasure

through me, his cock filling me repeatedly, over and over. Somehow, the feeling only intensifies, and I dig my nails into Beast's back, doing my part to work as well. The muscles in my legs scream out for me to slow down, to take a break, but I refuse. Not when he makes my head swim with joy. Not when I'm so wet for him, practically wetting the fur around the base of his erection.

"I knew it," he growls in my ear. The sound sends goosebumps through me once again, prickling my arms and thighs with excitement.

I can barely get it out, but I manage to ask, "Knew what?"

"I knew you'd look this beautiful on my cock," he says. "Knew you could take every bit of me. Knew how tight this sweet cunt would be."

It's filthy, the kind of lewd talk I'd expect to hear from men in town, but there's something different about the way it sounds now. How arousing it is to know that Beast spent nights imagining himself between my legs, not with his mouth but with something thicker. Harder.

I wrap my legs around his waist and squeeze tight, cupping his face in my hands and staring into his eyes. "How often did you think about me?" I ask.

His hands dig into my ass as he bounces me on him, drawing out a long moan from within me.

"Every night," he pants. "Every night, I dreamed of you. Kissing you. Licking you. Fucking you. And after all of it, filling you."

My back arches, and we're both chest to chest, me clinging to him as he thrusts his hips forward. At this angle, my clit is against him, and I buck my hips forward, that perfect, deliciously sweet spot stimulated just right. He purrs like he knows what I'm feeling.

"Fuck, Beast," I cry, my stomach tightening, every muscle clenching. I can feel it, just on the horizon, the sun rising over the crest of the hills. I want it, *need* it, and I chase it down with every ounce of focus I have. My hips find the perfect rhythm with Beast, jutting forward every time he slides me down his cock.

My toes curl, and my breathing grows labored, but it's not until Beast growls in my ear that I'm sent tumbling over the edge.

"Come for me, Isla. Show me how good I make your cunt feel."

A silent cry cuts through my throat, and I feel everything inside of me come to life, a swell of pleasure that leaves me physically shaking in his arms. Were it not for the way Beast holds me, my head would surely loll back, eyes squeezed tight, and my mouth parted in total satisfaction.

God.

Fuck.

I could cry; it feels so good. This reaction must be a compliment to Beast because he chuckles darkly and thrusts harder, faster. It takes all my strength not to go limp in his arms, but I manage, digging my nails into his back and fighting for control of myself once again.

"Make me yours, Beast," I plead, barely able to let out a string of words properly in the glow of my orgasm. I buck my hips against his, riding his cock as best I can. It's difficult to keep up with him, but I'm dedicated to learning. Perfecting my skills.

He takes hold of my face in one hand, intensity flaming in his eyes. "You are mine," he says through gritted teeth.

That phrase would've put me off more than anything else were I the same girl from all those weeks ago. Had I just arrived, I would've argued that I'm no one's. That I'm my own. I still feel that way, but this is different. This isn't ownership that he's demanding. I'm sharing myself with him, giving him permission to touch me in ways very few men have ever had the chance to. Giving myself to him is a gift that I'm willing to share as often as he'd like.

"I'm yours," I say, leaning in to kiss him. Beast

breaks the kiss only a second later, hands gripping my skin as his hips snap forward roughly.

"Fuck," he growls. "*Fuck*."

And then I feel him. His body tenses, violent shudders tearing through him as he reaches his climax. I press myself flat to him, practically dwarfed by his sheer size. His chest heaves against mine, and his stomach flexes repeatedly. The warmth of his seed inside of me is immediately recognized, and I smile against his pectoral muscle.

Beast presses me into the bed so quickly that my head spins again, and he thrusts a few more times, emptying the last of himself. I tighten my legs around his hips and hold him close, refusing to let go. Refusing to let him pull away and leave me empty again. Now that I've felt it, felt the completeness of him, I don't want to let it slip away.

Like all good things, it doesn't last forever. Beast slides free and pulls me into his arms, our heads against the pillows. That vicious, animalistic gaze he regarded me with is nowhere to be found. Instead, those eyes are soft now. Comforting. I could lie like this forever, wrapped in his embrace as we both come down from such a euphoric feeling. There's a stillness to the room, and everything from the night before disappears. No anxious churning in my stomach at the thought of Jacob and Wil. No anger toward Beast.

I know it's still there. I know that right now, more powerful emotions have come to the fore, but when I eventually lay my head down to sleep, those thoughts will return, haunting me and keeping me from peacefulness. But for the moment, I'm happy. For the moment, I relish in the afterglow of sex with Beast. This is tranquility. *He* is tranquility.

At least for a moment. Beast nuzzles into my hair, breathing deeply. "Do you know how incredible you are?" he asks in a low voice.

I close my eyes and smile, turning into his touch. "Perhaps just a bit."

"You're something else. Something special." He kisses the top of my head, then begins peppering down my cheek until eventually, he reaches my lips. There, his kisses turn deeper. More passionate.

"Are you tired?" I ask him. What I really mean is, does he have enough energy for more than just one go at all of this?

Beast must know exactly what I'm thinking because one hand slides from my shoulders down to my hips and between my legs. I gasp at the feeling of him penetrating me. He doesn't go too deep, just enough to stroke that particularly sensitive spot inside me, and I moan.

"Do I feel tired to you?" he smirks.

I bite my lip and grind my hips down against him. "No."

"I'll never get tired of you, my beauty."

Beast rolls me onto my back and hikes my hips up. He fucks me two more times, and just when I think he's finally worn himself out, he parts my legs and cleans up his messes.

"**A**m I allowed to ask where we're going?" I ask him, tripping over my feet as I blindly follow him through the halls of Highburn. He covers my eyes with one massive paw, obscuring my vision and making it only slightly more difficult to move around. Still, I don't complain much. This morning, Beast seems to have a new energy about him. He's anxious, but in that unease, he seems resolved, especially the way he says,

"No, that will ruin the surprise."

"So, it's a surprise for me?"

"In a way, yes."

His answer only leaves me with more questions, but I bite them back and allow him to lead me further through the castle. When we stop, his hand doesn't move from my eyes, but I do hear him push open a heavy set of doors.

"Here we are," he says softly.

I blink in the harsh sunlight once his hand is gone, squinting to get a good look at the room I've found myself in. I don't know where in the castle we are, and something tells me that's on purpose. The locks on the door do a good job of explaining why this room isn't public knowledge.

I step inside, taking in all of the shelves full of books. Leather-bound and weathered, I've never seen anything more beautiful. Father could never afford books of this quality. Anything Elyse and I read growing up was fragile, paper sewn together far too delicately for young girls to handle. I dreamed of owning a collection like this, of spending hours by myself, escaping into the world of kings and queens, fairies and goblins, and dragons and knights.

"It's beautiful," I whisper, but that doesn't even begin to cover it. Once the shock of the shelves wears off, I notice the glass cases hanging on the wall, each of them filled with various weapons. Longswords with intricate designs worked into the handles. Crossbows gleaming with a shine to rival diamonds. Lances, mauls, and flails. It's an arsenal of supplies. One could easily win a war with all these instruments of destruction. Suddenly, the tiny poniard I keep beneath my skirts seems so unimpressive.

"What is all of this for?" I ask, approaching the cases. Each piece is finely crafted with the initials G.L. inscribed on the handles. They're as breath-taking as the other pieces of artwork hanging on the walls of this massive castle.

"This was my father's study," he says, stepping in after me. Beast joins me in front of one of the winged spears and taps the glass right where the initials are. "Gregor Lovell."

"He must have really loved to fight," I comment, glancing up at Beast. He smiles humorlessly.

"One might think. No, the only thing Gregor Lovell loved was his own ego. He would often show our guests to this room and tell incredible stories of all the times he'd had to use one of these weapons to defend us. And when the guests were gone, and he'd swallowed so much wine that he couldn't stand up straight, he'd scream and shout and hit us. Gregor loved to collect things, but he never had the heart to wield any of these."

I've never met the man, yet I want to punish him for what he did to Beast and his mother, Rose. The way he treated them was cold. The actions of a coward, not a provider.

"Have you ever used them?"

Beast shakes his head and walks away from the glass cases. "No. I have no need."

I blush. Of course, he doesn't. I witnessed the way he handled the wolves that night. There's no need for swords or bludgeoning weapons when he has those razor-sharp claws and a set of teeth that could easily tear a man's throat out.

I continue around the room for a long while, dragging my fingers over the spines of aged books and even pulling a few out to examine the titles. None that I've ever heard of, but that only excites me more. So much unexpected joy could lie between the covers of each of these.

"Can I read these?" I ask, looking up to find him staring back at me with that quiet, pensive look on his face.

"Of course. That's why I brought you here. Well, not those books, really." He steps aside to reveal a desk with a stack of books on top. These are different than all the others. These seem more hastily made—as if someone from East Graybrook opened up a shop that he spent some time looking through.

"What are these?" I return the book in my hand to the shelf and approach the desk.

"Just...read them. Please. And when you're finished, come find me."

He starts to leave, but I catch his hand, stopping

him. Beast's eyes fall to my thin fingers wrapped around his.

"You'll be fine, my beauty. Just read them, and you'll understand why I brought you here. Try not to take too long; it's only a bit of light reading."

Beast's joke catches me off-guard, and I laugh softly. "Okay."

"Good. I'll see you soon."

The wooden doors rattle when Beast shuts me off from the rest of the world, reminding me of the first time he brought me to my room. It doesn't even feel like he's the same person as he was then. *I* don't feel like the same person. I'm not entirely sure I know what kind of person I am at all. Rather than having a small anxiety attack over that thought, I turn to the books, reaching for a red leather one and wiping away a thin layer of dust.

There's a small chair beside the desk, and I fold myself into it, cracking open the book and looking for an author. After a moment of searching, I realize that this isn't a book. It's a journal. A quick flip through the rest of the stack reveals the same information. All journals, all handwritten. The writing is a bit more difficult to decipher in the beginning, but I recognize the tone of voice without a shadow of a doubt.

These are Beast's journals.

The first one dates back to years ago. He must have been younger than me because his handwriting is barely legible. Checking my mental timeline, he must have only recently been cursed by the sorceress who left him in this state. That would explain the jagged, uneven lettering and why he doesn't stay on the lines all that well.

The first entry is angry. So angry and so violent. He recounts how, if he had the chance to start over again, he would tear the witch's legs from her hips and leave her and the child to die. He recounts instances of villagers shooting arrows at him thinking he was some animal in the woods. The worst of all is the description of the way his father treated him. What was once cold disregard turned to vile hatred so toxic that it burned everyone around them, from Rose to the rest of the staff.

I can feel the pain in every ragged swipe of ink, and it breaks my heart.

I want to pull him into my arms and tell this version of Beast that he will one day learn to cope with this new life of his. That yes, many will fear him, but there will be those that understand his anguish and empathize with him.

When I reach the end of the first entry, I see a

name. Of course, he would sign with his name. This was before he accepted the monster title. Before he let the world turn him into the one thing he never wanted to be. Still, seeing his name innocently scribbled at the bottom makes my heart twist.

He's not Beast.

Not the monster of Highburn Hold.

He's Lowen.

His words are enrapturing, and when I finish the first book, I reach for the second, diving deeper into his thoughts and his experiences. The way he felt when his mother passed brings tears to my eyes, and for a long time, I can't read any further. This wound we share makes me feel close to him, like he understands me, more than any man I might meet in East Graybrook.

I know the stares of the villagers. The way they whisper behind your back, some of them not even bothering to spare you the humiliation of leaving before they gossip. I know how harsh they can be to those who are different. They treated me with the same level of contempt.

Beast understands.

Lowen understands.

I swallow hard when I make my first appearance in his journals.

"I don't know what to make of this woman. I want to shake her, to scare her the same way I scared her pathetic father. Watching him cower was the very thing I needed. But this woman and the way she held herself. How she stared me in my eyes and told me that I didn't scare or intimidate her. I've made grown men piss their pants with a single roar, but not Isla.

Worst, she knew me better than I knew myself in that moment. Knew that, despite my physical appearance, I am a man with desires. And though many of the men I've captured have tried—and come close—to fully providing that satisfaction, I know that she might give me what I've craved for so long. I know it. She knows it. That's why she offered herself.

I should kill her. That's the smart option. Kill my temptation. Remain steadfast in the life I've led for so long. Things are good here. None of my servants step out of line. No one bothers me. Having this woman here would threaten all of that.

But I can't do it. I can't bring myself to do it. Not to a creature so carefully crafted by God. To lay a finger on her would be an affront to every holy being. A slash across one of my priceless paintings.

Maybe that's the reason I thought about slipping that gown from her shoulders and having my way with her."

I'd like to think that I'm not the shy type, but reading about the way Beast thought of me makes my stomach twist into giddy knots. Even more, arrogance bubbles in my chest with the knowledge that I wasn't easy for him. There are so many things in life I'd like for the man I care about to think of me, but manageable is not one of them.

My mother gave my father hell until the day she passed, and he loved her even more for it.

I don't stop reading through Beast's journals until I make it to the last page. I trace my fingers over every perfect loop and slash of his letters. His penmanship is excellence, but better than that are his sentiments.

"There is not much I fear in this world. I've known death. I've known suffering. I've played my part in both equally. The one thing I do fear is that soon, my beauty will discover the power she holds over me, and she will strike me down with it. She will bring me to my knees, unlike any other, and she will not hesitate to finish me.

I wait every moment for her to make that decision. I wring my hands over the thoughts that so ruthlessly mock me. She could never love someone as tainted as me. She would rather die than be mine. By her own blade or the gnashing teeth of wolves in the trees.

I don't deserve the patience she's given me. I don't

deserve the compassion she's shown me. Not when I so heartlessly imprisoned her in my home. Ripped from her family, she can only harbor hate in her heart for me. Yet, if this is how she feels, she does a good job of concealing it.

I may never know her true emotions, but I know that I must convince her. If it takes handing her a blade and telling her to do her worst, I will. And if she were to push that blade through my chest and take my life, it will have been worth it. To know someone as wholly incomparable as my Isla is a gift I would die one thousand times over for."

A large tear splatters against the page, smearing the ink. I wipe my eyes hastily, dabbing off the wetness on the paper with the sleeve of my dress, sniffing hard. I don't know what to say or even what to think. I don't force it, either. Instead, I toss the last journal onto the desk and leap from the chair, flinging the doors open and racing down the hallway.

He is in his room, and his head snaps up the second I burst through the doors. He's just stood up by the time I launch myself into his arms. He laughs softly, somewhat mildly nervous, and says,

"Hello to you as well."

I want to think of something intelligent to say, but the only words that escape me are, "I love you."

Beast looks at me with confusion carved into his face. "What?"

"I love you, Lowen. I...I love you."

There's nothing else to say. Nothing else feels right other than this. For so long, I wanted to deny it. Pretend that it was something else. Pity for the cursed man in the frightening castle all alone. Me taking back power from a man that took it from me. But the truth is, it's all of that and more. It's an intricate web of hatred and sadness and fire-hot love. I want to hold him and protect him and push him down onto his bed and fuck him until neither of us can move.

"Isla," he says, but before another word slips free, I press my lips to his.

"No," I say when the kiss ends. "Don't ask me if I mean it. Don't ask me if I'm sure. If I wasn't sure, I would have left last night. But I'm here, Lowen. I'm here, and I'm admitting that I love you."

"It just doesn't seem right," he breathes. "It doesn't make sense to me how you could choose me after everything that I've done."

"I don't understand how either, Lowen, but I know that it's the truth."

He cups my face in his large hands and smiles at me, eyes full of something no man has ever looked at me with. "I love you, Isla. God, I love you."

Another slow kiss follows, and when I press him down to the bed, he doesn't fight me.

I don't leave that bed for the rest of the night.

Not until we've both proven how we truly feel, again and again.

And again.

❧ 14 ❧

The winter air is dry enough to wake me from my sleep, my itching throat crying out for water. As quietly as I can, I slip out from beneath Lowen's arms and pad down the hall. The chill freezes my toes, so I move quickly, hurrying down the stairs until I make it to the kitchen. Our evening of laughter, wine, and dinner left me too drunk to change out of my golden evening dress before collapsing into bed with Lowen, but even that's not enough to help with the temperatures.

The castle is quiet enough to hear even the littlest of breaths from the mice, and locating a mug sounds like I've joined a traveling musician's group with all the noise I'm making. I finally sink a mug into the bronze bucket of water one of the servants brought up from the river earlier in the day, carrying it to the dining room to sit and drink.

If I'd felt a shift in the air the first night I spent with Lowen, this new change feels like the kind of wind that rattled the wooden shutters of my childhood home and shook the building down to its core. It doesn't feel real, but I know that this is my situation.

I've fallen in love with the beast.

No, that's not quite right. I've fallen for a man cursed from his beastly actions. He's not the result of his mistakes, just as I'm not a combination of all the terrible things I've done. Lowen is a man as complex as any other, but despite all his flaws and shortcomings, I love him more than I've loved any other man. Though there haven't been many, this is the feeling I believed I'd found. All the times I'd proclaimed my affections pale in comparison.

Elyse won't understand it. Were I in her shoes, I wouldn't understand it. How could someone moderately well-adjusted make this decision? Would any sane woman choose to sleep with the beast of this castle over a man from East Graybrook?

That voice is getting quieter, but she's still there. She tells me that I've fallen for my captor. But the louder side, the one that feels closer to my heart than my brain, argues that with Lowen, I've never felt this much freedom. Freedom from struggle, from wondering where my next meal will come from. Worrying over Father as he heads out on another run for money. Every wish I could ever make will be granted here, by a man who has so many times shown me that he will do whatever it is that I ask. This is the fairy tale my mother told me about, and I should savor it. Ignore the negative thoughts warning me that at any moment, something will go wrong and shatter this illusion I've allowed to cloud my vision.

I finish the last of my water and shake my head, running fingers through slightly tangled hair. If this is all temporary, the best I can do is make the most of it. Try to find some way to help Elyse. Do my best to take the gifts I've received from Lowen and do good in this world while I still can. Resolved, I sit up straight and take a deep, slow breath.

I rise to put away my mug, but the strangest little flicker of orange through the glazed windows of the dining room catch my eye. I pause and tilt my head, narrowing my eyes to get a better look. The orange orb grows larger, multiplying and splitting off into smaller speckles of vibrant color. Curiously, I set down my mug and approach the window.

The lights dance across the darkness like fireflies, still growing larger and larger. Accompanying the light, though, is the sound of distant voices. Deep, rumbling voices that only increase in volume the closer those flickers get. I step back from the window when there's enough light to illuminate what exactly I'm looking at.

It's not one or two men but rather a small army, armed with torches and a variety of weapons. Swords hang from the backs of some while other men in the group grip the handles of pitchforks with weathered, dirty fingers. Their voices are deep and rowdy, some shouting while the rest murmur in agreement. There's almost a drunken cadence to the way they speak like ale has given power to their anger.

Every hair on the back of my neck stands up, and I retreat from the window, my heart leaping into my throat. I don't know what's happening, but I know that it's nothing good. In my experience, no collection of men that loud and upset can bring anything other than trouble. As quietly as I can, I hurry to the foyer. The men still have distance to cover before they make it to the door, so I spare another peek out into the darkness.

Their faces are almost indistinguishable in the orange glow of their torches, but the sight of one rips an involuntary cry from my throat. I recognize the gash across his face, from one corner of his lip up to his ear.

"Lowen!" I almost don't recognize my own scream. "Lowen!"

In seconds, I can hear him racing toward me. He makes it to the top of the staircase and pauses, head scanning the room. "Isla? What? What's wrong?"

I can't bring myself to explain the situation. No matter how hard I try to form the words, I only find myself shaking, trembling at the thought that somehow Wil survived our fight. Somehow, he made it home quickly enough to have his wounds tended to. I can only point to the window.

Lowen leaps from the stairs and rushes to the glass, looking out at the mob. "What in God's name?" he says quietly. Behind me, I can hear shuffling, and I look back to see Mrs. Potter and Charlie rubbing sleep from their eyes.

"What's going on?" Mrs. Potter asks.

"I'm not sure," Lowen replies absently. His eyes don't leave the window, and I can tell by the hunch of his shoulders and the slow creeping of his claws extending that he's acutely aware of the same thing I am. These men aren't here to talk. They're not here for any benign reason.

We stand side by side as the men approach the castle, but they don't stop at the steps. They march up to the door and pound angry fists against it. It's a childish, fearful thought, but for the briefest moment, I imagine them knocking down the wooden doors and rushing inside.

"Nana," Charlie whimpers, clinging to Mrs. Potter's nightgown. She wraps a comforting arm around him, but the expression on her face mirrors my own.

"Open these fucking doors," a raspy voice shouts from the other side. He follows his order with another hard knock.

"What do we do?" I ask Lowen in a hushed tone. I don't want to scare Mrs. Potter or Charlie, and I force myself to swallow down the terror clawing up the back of my throat. Keep it together. Think this through. That's all we have to do.

Lowen opens his mouth to speak, but he's cut off by an explosion of noise. The shattered glass bounces to the stone floor below, and a heavy rock rolls a few feet before stopping. I cover my mouth, and Lowen growls, racing to the doors and swinging them open wildly. Before the men can say anything, he roars, sending the few at the front of the mob staggering backward.

"You dare damage my property?" Lowen asks. "I should tear each of you limb from limb."

Wil's eyes harden, and he steps forward. "Just like you did to my brother?" he asks.

"I've never met your brother in my life," he challenges, stepping closer.

"You killed him, and now you deny it," Wil insists, reaching for his weapon. He unsheathes a sword, and moonlight glints off the tip of it. "You are under arrest, you beast. I would suggest you don't make this any more difficult." That garners a few shouts of approval. They want to detain him for something he didn't do. Something that was my fault.

"It was me," I say. "I killed your brother."

A ripple of murmurs rolls through the mob, but Wil says, "No, it was this abomination."

"Why are you lying? I killed your brother, and I tried to kill you. You were going to attack me. It was self-defense."

He laughs cruelly and says, "Do I look like the type of man to be bested by some woman? Especially one like *you*?" His men laugh, and I feel that anger inside of me, stirring to life once more. Any other time, I would lull it back to sleep and convince myself to calm down, but I can't. Not when these bastards have scared the people I care about and damaged Lowen's property.

"You look better than the man I left in the woods that day when I cut his fucking face open and left him there to bleed out." All at once, that laughter is cut short.

"It's clear she's delusional," Wil says to his men. "We should take her in as well. For working with this monster. For fornicating with an animal." That's what seems to rile his mob up more than anything else. The idea that I could ever find enjoyment from Lowen. That, to be in love with a man like him, I must be unstable. Their jeers grow louder, and they spit vile insults at the both of us, their anger swelling with no signs of stopping.

"We'll take them both," one man cries.

"Don't even take them," another adds. "Just get rid of them now."

"I say we kill both of them and anyone else that is working with him."

That's when I notice the shift in Lowen's demeanor. What was once morbid curiosity is now an anger I've only seen once, in the woods. The rational side of him takes a step back, and now someone else is in charge. It's not Lowen standing before this mob, but the Beast.

The arrow moves so quickly that I don't notice it until Beast lets out a grunt and stumbles back. I blink, glancing at him. The projectile sticks out from his shoulder, and though I'm sure it must sting, it looks comically small compared to the breadth of his build. I start to reach for the arrow when something hard connects with my head, and I'm knocked off-kilter, falling to the ground beside the rock thrown at me.

"Oh, God," Mrs. Potter cries as she and Charlie rush toward me.

The world spins for a moment, but the bone-rattling roar that tears through the foyer snaps me back into alertness. I turn to the door in time to see the men approaching, at least thirty of them, entering the castle with one thing on their minds.

Wil looks between me and Lowen, a smirk on his face and his knuckles white as he grips his sword.

"Kill them," he says simply.

The mob, like one snarling, angry sentient being, rushes forward at the same time.

❧ 15 ❧

always told myself that I didn't fear death. That I *wouldn't* fear death. When it's my time to go, there's nothing I can do to stop it. It was easy to hold that confidence from such a considerably sheltered life. I'd never been forced to fight in a war waged by some money-hungry monarch. I'd never put my life on the line every single day. That kind of self-congratulatory arrogance was easy to uphold from the safety of my home.

Now, I fear death.

Not just for myself, but the people that I care about. The servants of Highburn. The Beast of Highburn. I fear death as it marches through the doors of the castle, blades drawn and fire in its eyes. It's coming for us, and I'm afraid.

The foyer is filled with chaos, a cacophony of

noise that builds so intensely and immediately that it almost doesn't feel real. The roaring booming from Beast's throat as he leaps seven feet forward, feet planted on the chest of one man as he knocks him to the ground. The shouts from the mob, swords clanking as they arm themselves and charge. Mrs. Potter and the other servants screaming in terror.

I lie frozen on the floor, helpless to move.

Helpless to react.

Witnessing the servants being attacked doesn't shake me, nor does the sound of spattering gore as Beast's claws slash through the throats of two men, decorating the stone with bright red showers. It's not until I scan the nightmarish scene and focus in on Charlie that my body finally agrees with me. A large man with a dagger approaches him, towering over the little boy. Mrs. Potter tries to intervene, but he swiftly delivers a slap to the face that sends her colliding into a suit of armor, toppling it.

"Get away from him," I whisper, scrambling up from my knees and racing toward them. I dodge two different men lunging at me and throw my entire weight into the man just as he grabs a fistful of Charlie's shirt. The three of us smack against the ground hard, and I grab for the man's fingers, trying to pry them open long enough for Charlie to escape.

The man yanks my head back by my hair, trying

to keep his grip on Charlie while pulling me away. Rather than tugging at his hands, I pivot to his face, pounding my fists against him until he finally lets Charlie free and strikes me in retaliation. With both hands, he tosses me off of him. The landing knocks the wind out of me, but I roll onto my side, relieved to see Charlie running to Mrs. Potter.

"There the bitch is," the man chuckles darkly, licking blood from his teeth and gums as he approaches. I crawl backward away from him, frantically searching for something to use to protect myself. A fallen blade disregarded in the attack surrounding us. I only find puddles of oozing blood and broken glass.

"Don't run now," he says, his speed quickening. "You're lucky; I like when women fight back. Makes it more fun to—"

The downward swing of the axe cuts through his words the same as it cuts through the top of his skull. He pauses, blinking twice with his mouth hanging open. He tries to force out the last few words but drops to his knees instead. Mrs. Potter stands behind him, gasping, her face already bruised from being smacked around.

I want to thank her for saving me, but I have to return the favor first. We have to get Charlie and the rest of the servants out of here before anyone else is hurt. She helps pull me from the ground, and I throw my arms around her for a brief hug.

"Follow me," I say, turning to Charlie and hefting him up into my arms. The tears in his eyes soak through my dress immediately, and I run my fingers through his hair. "It's okay," I whisper, racing down the back halls of the castle. Mrs. Potter follows close behind, trailed by other maids, cooks, and groundskeepers.

"We're almost there," I promise, trying my best to retrace my footsteps the first time I walked through these halls. I get turned around once, but eventually, I push through the doors of the dungeon. We're immediately hit with a cold blast of air, but this time, it's comforting. It's a way out of these walls that these men don't have any idea of.

When I set Charlie down, he runs to Mrs. Potter. I turn to Henry and Eve, both of whom have taken a beating, and say,

"Do not open this door for anyone you don't know, do you understand? Stay here. Don't make a sound. If I don't come back for you before sunrise, you have to escape." I point across the room, and all eyes follow my gesture. "That's your way out. It's going to be cold, but if you stick together, you can make it to East Graybrook on foot in an hour or so."

Henry nods, but Eve only says, "Where are you going?"

"I have to help Lowen," I say. "He can't fight them all on his own."

"This is your chance to get away," a man in the back of the room says. "This is a chance for all of us."

I want to scream at him for thinking of leaving, but I can't. All the horrible things Lowen must have subjected them to in all his years of being this way is so different from my experience. To fault them for something I had the privilege of avoiding would be wrong.

"Then leave," I say earnestly. "Make your escape. I'm not going to stop you, but I won't be joining you. This is my home. This is where I want to be, and I'm going to defend it with the man that I love."

There's no more time to talk. I give Henry and Eve a look, they nod, and then I leave them in the dungeon, closing the door behind me. I squeeze my eyes shut hard and whisper a silent prayer. I beg that God protects them, that He shows them mercy and doesn't make their lives any harder than He already has. They don't deserve any of this.

"Amen," I whisper. Now I have to go.

I race down the halls of the castle with one room in mind. The room I realized I loved Lowen Lovell in. The room that will help me save him.

Gregor's study is dark, but I don't need much light to see where I need to go. I reach the glass cases and scan through my options, quickly deciding on the longsword. I use one of the books to smash the glass and quickly lift it from the rack, steadying it in my hands. It's lighter than I thought, and when I grip it in both hands and swing, my stomach roils with something.

Determination? Fury?

There's no time to decipher the physical response. Making quick work, I cut at the billowing fabric of my gown until there's room to move easily, no longer forced to hike up my skirts in order to run. I wish I had taken the armor from earlier, and I kick myself for not thinking ahead. No matter. There's no time to replay the scene in my head. Not when Lowen is in danger.

I ignore the sharp chill on the soles of my feet, pressing forward until I reach the dining hall. There, I pause, watching as two cooks stand over a sputtering man lying flat on his back. The knives in their hands drip with blood. I start to pass them when one of the men jumps, knife drawn, ready to strike.

"Oh," he says, panting with relief.

"The others are in the dungeon. Tell them that I sent you there. If these men come, you need to protect them, okay?"

"Yes, Miss Isla," the other, heftier man says. The two of them head in the opposite direction, back where I came from. Before I can leave, the bleeding attacker on the floor grabs my ankle weakly. I stare down at his hand, then into his eyes.

"Kill me," he pleads. His voice is raspy. "Please, kill me."

"No."

With a quick jerk of my leg, I kick his hand off and leave him to bleed out, jogging through the doors of the castle to find the carnage waiting for me in the foyer. Corpses are strewn from end to end, arms ripped from torsos, bones jutting out, in angles that don't look right. One of the bodies has its face smashed in, the back of the head uncomfortably flush with the stone floor beneath it.

And Lowen.

He's drenched in gore, gray and white fur stained red, and hunched over at a small group of men with swords drawn. One fires from his crossbow, and it pierces through Lowen's leg. His howl sends vibrations through my body, and when he snarls and slashes at the men, they scurry back, putting more distance between them. He has it under control.

But that changes the second I see one of the bodies move. He lifts his head, checking that the coast is clear before he slides out from beneath a fallen friend and rises. He quietly grabs his spear and steadies himself on his feet, approaching with the silence of someone trained to kill. The words stick to the back of my throat, and I act before I can speak.

I can see the whole scene unfolding before me. Lowen, oblivious to the wolf creeping up on him. The man taking aim and putting all of his weight into the spear as he pierces Lowen from behind. Watching the love of my life bleed out before the mob turns its attention to me.

No.

No.

Though the blood-soaked stones are slick, I tear over them in an all-consuming anger and clench both hands around the hilt of the sword, holding it against my hip. He lifts his spear and arches his hand back. I only have seconds. Another booming roar cuts through the room, but it's not Lowen. It's not the men ready to kill him.

It's me.

"No," I howl. The noise makes the man jump, and he looks over his shoulder just as I lunge forward and force the sword through his back. The noise is nauseating, a loud pop following the initial wet squish. The sword appears on the other side of him, drenched in blood as it pokes through his chest, just beneath his ribcage.

The world seems to halt for just one moment, all eyes on us. Lowen spins around to stare at me, his golden eyes flickering between me and the man that almost took his life. The one raising his spear once again, ready to use his last bit of strength. Lowen glances at the sword, at me, and then back at the sword.

"Do it," I say, and he moves without hesitation.

Lowen lifts his massive leg, and I tighten my grip on the hilt just as he stomps down on the end of the blade protruding from the other side of this would-be assassin. I drop my weight with Lowen, and together, the sword tears through the man, finally free once it exits between his legs.

A slurry of organs spills from the wound, splattering against the floor in a sickeningly wet, glimmering pile of carnage. The man's grip loosens around the handle of his spear, and he drops forward, face-first, onto the ground.

"Jesus," one of the men watching us whispers. It's enough to break me out of the shock of doing this. Lowen pulls me to him for a brief hug.

"You're okay," he murmurs.

Though my voice is shaky, I manage to get out, "What, you didn't think I was capable?"

"A rose with her thorns," he says, pressing a kiss to my head.

If I could, I'd stay here forever in this moment, relieved to know that Lowen is okay. That we're okay. But we're not finished yet. I pull away from Lowen's arms and grab my longsword from the ground, wiping the blood off on my dress.

Wil and the last remaining men in his mob stare at me as I approach them. "You wanted to kill the Beast of Highburn Hold," I remind them. "Come, kill us."

"You fucking bitch," Wil screeches, raising his sword and charging at me rather than Lowen like the other men do. He wants me dead like it's his life's purpose. He came here for this very reason. Only one of us will live—but it won't be him.

His first swing is easy to duck under, but when Wil quickly retaliates with a jab, the edge of his blade catches my bare shoulder. It sends a sharp heat of pain through my arm, and I let out a cry of pain, just barely dodging another quick jab. Satisfaction drips from his smile like slobber, and the stitches on his cheek strain so wide that I'm certain they're going to tear.

Wil doesn't give me a moment to regain my balance before he launches another attack, this time swinging for my feet. I throw myself backward and let him stumble forward from his own momentum before I strike back, arcing my sword down to his thigh. It tears through like warm butter, and he shouts in pain.

The sword nearly slips from my hand as I go in for another swipe, but I land it across his chest. Wil howls, a wounded animal, no longer capable of rational thought. Murder glimmers in his dark eyes, and he catches me off-guard by grabbing hold of my sword, directly on the blade, and jerking it away, sending it clattering toward the staircase.

"We should've just killed you on the road," he huffs, using his now-wounded hand to brush the hair back from his face. "Should've cut your fucking head off when we had the chance."

I fall back, retreating to give myself enough room to dodge anything else he sends my way. Out of the corner of my eye, I can see Lowen reach for one of the mobsters and dig both sets of claws into his chest. He rips his hands free, and before the man hits the ground, he's dead.

"You should've killed me, you're right," I say to Wil, stumbling over a body behind me. "Maybe then, your pathetic rapist of a brother would still be here."

"Fuck you," he screams, dashing toward me and jabbing my way. I leap back, panting hard.

"You know, it should've been you to go first," I taunt. "Do you see how many people you needed to even come close to taking me down? Jacob didn't need an army. He almost had me all on his own. Like a man. You, though? Not even close."

"You shut your fucking mouth!" Wil's anger has overtaken him, and he reacts on instinct, slashing wildly. I throw myself to the floor and scramble for the hard metal beneath me, raising the piece of armor just in time to block a blow aimed directly at my head.

Wil is caught off-guard, and I kick my leg up hard, connecting with his crotch. He lets out a sharp grunt and drops down to his knees. My grip tightens around the chest plate in my hand, and I swing wide, slamming it against his face. This sends Wil down to the ground, flat on his back.

Like before, there's no witty retort that springs to mind. I think of nothing but murder as I straddle him and raise the piece of armor high over my head. Everything else around me disappears as I focus on smashing the metal against his face again and again and again. I don't stop until I'm sure he's dead, and even then, I hit him even harder.

Wil's twitching stops, and when I pull the armor away, there's nothing recognizable about his face. My muscles scream as I drop the weapon and climb off of him, and I find myself panting like some kind of exhausted animal.

Discarding the armor, I grab my sword from the

stairs and turn back to see Lowen with his massive teeth buried in a man's shoulder, shaking him wildly, from right to left. His feet swing as he tries to fight it, but when Lowen tosses him into the wall, his head twists at an odd angle, and a loud, sick crunch echoes through the room. His body hits the floor like a sack of flour.

Lowen starts for the last man cowering in the corner, but I beat him there, giving him a knowing look before I turn to the man. He can't be older than seventeen, not even a man. There's a side of me that pities him for getting swept up in all of this. Then I recall the way they so willingly came to kill me and Lowen. How his friends hurt Mrs. Potter and Charlie. That momentary empathy evaporates.

I grab the boy by his shirt and give him a hard, quick shake. "Do you want to die?" I demand, the blade of my sword resting on his throat. I can practically feel his rapid pulse against the metal.

"N-no," he whimpers, tears brimming his eyes as they glance at the corpses surrounding us.

"Then you will never come back to Highburn Hold," I say. I drag him to the door. "Don't even *think* about walking through these doors again. If you do, I promise you; you won't have to worry about the beast. I will kill you before he even finds out you came back. Is that clear?"

He lets out a snotty wail and nods enthusiastically. Satisfied, I give him a hard push that sends him sprawling down the stairs outside. "Tell everyone in East Graybrook that they should all stay away. Any soul foolish enough to find themselves in my home will fare the same fate as the men here tonight."

The boy scrambles to his feet and takes off running, not once looking back at me.

Without another word, I slam the door closed.

I can hear Lowen's labored breathing, and I turn around, fully prepared to throw myself into his arms. He's doubled over, his frame rising and falling as he struggles to remain upright.

"Lowen," I start.

He collapses to the ground. In seconds, I'm on my knees beside him. Only then can I see the various arrows, slashes, and wounds peppered all over his body. His eyes flutter shut, and I scream his name, shaking him. He's not dead. He's not fucking dead. He can't be.

"Lowen!" I cry, my fists full of fur as I try to shove him awake.

His eyes stay closed.

❧ 16 ☙

I haven't left Lowen's side since the attack three nights ago. At first, Mrs. Potter tried to encourage me to get some sleep and let her take care of him, but I refused. I wouldn't leave him for anything. Not until I knew he was okay. Using the washroom was hard, and I found myself hurrying to finish my business before I returned to his side. Letting him out of my sight for even a second felt like a walk through the woods alone. Utterly terrifying.

Mrs. Potter and I tend to his wounds every few hours, changing out the bandages and cleaning him up. Were he just a man, I'm certain he would've been dead a long time ago. No human body could take this much abuse and still fight to stay alive.

But I know he's somewhere in there. Somewhere

fighting to come back to his castle. To his servants. To me.

That's why I refuse to start thinking of burial options despite there being murmurs throughout Highburn Hold. Several of the cooks and gardeners have been whispering, and though I want to snap at them and tell them he's not dead yet, I have to keep positive. The same way Elyse always expects the worst, I have to treat them kindly and gently. Assure them that even if their worst fears come to light, we'll be okay.

I don't know how. All of this is Lowen's. They all live in his home, and if he dies, where will they go? Can they stay here? Will I leave to live with Elyse again? I need another glass of Mrs. Potter's tea to help with the throbbing pain behind my eyes.

Downstairs, I bring water to a boil, ignoring offers from the cooks to take care of it. "I'm okay, thank you," I say, waving them away. I need to do this. To do something other than pace back and forth in Lowen's room, praying and pleading with God to let him live the same way I did the night of the attack.

When I walk through the foyer, I swear I can still smell the stench of death lingering in the air. It's thick, like some kind of sickly molasses that nothing will wash away. And if I close my eyes and think hard enough, I can imagine that scene of carnage with startling accuracy. I can retrace my steps and recall every corpse. Every heart ripped from its chest or eye gouged from its socket. I've been having nightmares again because of it.

But I'm still here because of that night. Because Lowen gave everything he had—to protect me and the people inside this castle. If this is the price I have to pay to still live, then I have no choice but to hand over every last coin to my name.

I stir in leaves and spices, watching the drink grow darker in pigment. The light golden color deepens into a rich brown shade, and that's when I know it's done. I fill a mug and carry it to the dining room, dropping down into the seat at the head of the table.

The thought crosses my mind that I should feel empowered by all of this. For all the world knows, I conquered the beast. Pulled myself from the depths of Lowen's dungeon and made it to the head of the table. Climbed so high that the servants all regard me with the same level of respect as Lowen. This should feel like victory.

The darkness in my ear whispers that I should pray for Lowen to remain unresponsive. All of this will be mine and my sister's.

Immediately, I fight back against that idea, scolding myself for even entertaining it for a second.

Standing above others has never been my goal. I was never raised to want more than others but rather to want all the same freedoms. All the same luxuries. I was taught that those that can help but simply don't are not the people we should look up to. The ones deserving of our admiration are the people that struggle but still, somehow, find a way to help the rest of their community.

I rise from my seat and stand beside the table. It's easier to finish my drink this way. As I gulp down the last bit of semi-sweet tea, Mrs. Potter comes running in, eyes wildly searching for something. They land on me, and she swallows a gulp of air to say,

"He's awake."

The mug in my hand clatters against the table as I let it fall. Under any other circumstance, I would take it back and wash it, but I can't be bothered. Not now. Mrs. Potter follows me up the stairs, right on my heels. She's talking, but none of the words register. The one thing on my mind is the fact that he's not gone. I don't quite believe her until I push through the doors and see him being tended to by one of his servants. He tries to wave her off, but she fights him, glaring at him until he lets her change the bandages.

The second our eyes meet, he starts to push himself up from the bed.

"No," I say, running to him, dropping down to my knees. "Don't get up. Rest."

Lowen is reluctant, but he eventually relaxes. "Leave us," he says to the rest of the women in the room. I nod at Mrs. Potter's curious glance to let her know that I'm okay. That I can handle this. After the others shuffle out of the room and close the door, it's just me and Lowen.

He cups my face with one massive hand, stroking my cheek gently. "You're okay," he murmurs. Not quite like he's surprised, but more that he's relieved. I don't know how either of us are still kicking. With all those men, we should've been dead.

"You're okay too," I say, looking him over. He doesn't look anywhere near as bad as he did the night of the attack, but he'll need quite a bit more time to fully recover.

"Somehow," he laughs. He then adds, "Not somehow. I'm okay because of you. I'm *alive* because of you."

"I could say the same for you."

"It wouldn't be true," he says. He leans forward and presses his forehead to mine. I can feel the heat flooding through him, and I close my eyes, fighting back tears. There aren't words to describe the way this feels, and though I could try, it would all pale in comparison to the reality. My love is still alive. He'll recover. *We'll* recover.

"I was so worried about you," he says. "God only knows what those men would have done. I had to protect you. But you...you saved me in the end. Had you not been there, that man would have killed me."

My mind flashes back to the way my sword felt going through his back. How satisfying it was, watching his body empty out onto the floor between his legs. The beauty and the horror of it. Does that make me sick? No rational person in this world would find pleasure in that, yet here I am, pleased that it was him to die and not Lowen.

"Do you think they'll come back?" I ask, pulling back to look at him. His golden eyes are on fire, searching mine.

"Maybe. I'm not sure."

"If they're smart, they won't." There's an edge to my voice. A flip in my tone. Before that night, I would have been afraid. I would've cowered away at the idea of intruders coming to harm Lowen and the servants I've come to love. But that woman is nowhere to be found. Someone else has now stepped into her shoes, assumed her position. I don't quite know who she is right now, but she's my strength. The reassurance that no matter what happens, I will fight for Lowen the same way he will fight for me.

"If they're smart, they'll leave us to ourselves. Unless they'd like to join their friends in their graves."

Lowen's brow bone rises in surprise. "Perhaps it's time to retire 'my beauty.' What do you say, my beast?"

I scrunch up my nose and laugh at his new, terrible nickname. "I prefer 'my beauty.'"

His laughter is music to my ears. "I do, too. My rose, maybe?"

"Okay," I say, nodding slowly. "I like that."

"My rose." He repeats it once more, looking quite pleased with himself. "God, I love you," he says. He pulls me in for a kiss. We don't stop kissing, not even when my eyes well with thick tears of relief. I crawl into bed with him, right by his side.

He feels like home. Being by his side feels like I know my place. Not held hostage in his terrifying dungeon or beautiful guest rooms, but in bed, beside him. Equals. When I look at him, I know that he sees someone else sitting next to him. I'm no longer the beautiful prize he captured, but the woman that saved his life. The woman that fought to protect his castle when he needed help. The woman that nursed him back to health.

When I look into his eyes, Lowen stares back at me. Appreciative. Grateful. Enamored.

Lowen drifts off to sleep not long after, and I

stroke my fingers through his fur. Trace the curves of his horns with my fingertips. Somehow, in his sleep, Lowen looks like a smaller animal, peacefully resting. His broad chest expands and contracts with every breath, hypnotically rhythmic.

It's now that I decide that I don't care if they come back or not.

If they do, if they bring back an even bigger army of men to try to take us down, we'll kill them.

We'll kill anyone who threatens to harm us or the servants. Anyone who poses a threat to our wellbeing. Maybe that makes me a monster the same as Lowen. Maybe I've become just as detestable as the person who lies beside me, stitched and bandaged. If that's the truth, then so be it. Let me become a monster if it means protecting the people I love. Let them villainize me.

And if any of the villagers work up the nerve to come back up this hill with weapons and torches drawn, ready to wage another war, I hope they're prepared because there isn't just one beast of Highburn Hold.

There are two.

EPILOGUE

The smell of spring drifts through the open windows of Highburn Hold, filling the castle walls with daisies and roses and fresh grass. When it rouses me from my sleep, I yawn and stretch, rolling over to Lowen. He's not in bed, but I place my fingers on the dent in the sheets where he once was. It's still warm. He hasn't been gone for long.

I slip on my nightgown and pull my hair back, tying it with one of the many silk ribbons Lowen had delivered for my birthday weeks ago. Part of me thinks that I should spend the morning getting ready, putting on my best dress and finest jewelry for our guest later this afternoon. The other side tells me that she'll hate it if everything is stuffy and uncomfortable. It took me weeks to convince her in the first place.

I find Lowen down in the garden, helping the carpenters carry wooden logs to the tree line. It's so strange seeing him interacting with others. Before I met him, Mrs. Potter said that he'd never made an effort to talk to anyone in East Graybrook. He was a recluse, sending others to pick up his food and clothing. Communicating through letters rather than in person. If there was a way to avoid human contact, he would.

And now here he is, speaking with the small group of men I hired to help build the rest of the cabins for our staff. Lowen fought me in the beginning, insisting that none of his employees minded having to make the journey from their homes up to the castle every week. They liked having their own space. His perspective quickly changed when I brought him down to Mrs. Potter's downtrodden little home.

The place wasn't safe for adults, let alone children Charlie's age. That was when he finally agreed to let me hire men to create individual cabins for any servant that wanted to stay on the property. They wouldn't have to pay to live, and they also would have their wages increased, yet another thing that Lowen initially complained about.

His old, selfish habits are hard to kill, but I'm getting better at it. He's gentler. Kinder. Nowhere near as moody and brooding and brutal as he was before. He carries himself with more class, more dignity, too, like he's somehow become more esteemed since I agreed to be his. And make no mistake, that beast is still in there. When I need him to be rough around the edges and give me what I need, he's more than happy to. More than happy to be the man I want to father my babies.

We've tried—quite often, and quite enthusiastically—but sadly, it's likely not in our future. It must be for the best. I'm not even sure what our child would look like. Who it would take after. Maybe we'll find a baby on our doorstep like in all the stories my mother used to read to me. I know that Lowen will be a good father. One that will need me to smack him behind the head every now and again, but a good father regardless. One like my own.

When the sun is at its fullest in the sky, Mrs. Potter steps out into the garden and taps my shoulder. "She's here," she says once I turn to look at her.

I smile and thank her, excusing myself and racing to the front door. Elyse stands in the most stunning emerald dress I've ever seen her in, her golden hair swept up into a knot at the top of her head. She looks vibrant, so full of life, that I can't help but throw my arms around her and pull her in for a long hug.

"My goodness, look at you," I say when I pull back. "What happened?"

"I met someone," she says, beaming. Over her shoulder, I see a handsome man with short, black hair lifting bags from the back of a carriage. I don't recognize him, but from the way he dresses and the beautiful horses he has tugging his carriage, it's clear that he's wealthy.

"You have to tell me all about him," I whisper, glancing up at her lover as I guide her inside. It feels like we're girls again, giggling about boys that are just too dashing for their own good.

Truthfully, I've missed this more than anything else. Elyse was the second half of my heart, and when I asked Lowen to allow her to move in, it was the one thing he didn't hesitate to agree with. He wanted to meet her and apologize for all that he put us through. Opening his home to her and getting her out of the shack we'd spent all our lives in was the least he could do.

I lace my fingers through Elyse's and give her a full tour of the home while her lover, John, puts her belongings away in the old room I used to call my own. To my delight, she adores it instantly, and once we finish with the tour, she flops down onto the bed on her belly, groaning at how soft it is.

"I just can't believe you ever wanted to leave this place," she teases.

"Only because I missed you," I say. I take a seat beside her and drag my fingers through her hair. She looks so much like Mother that it oftentimes feels like staring at a twin. Mother used to say that about me, too. How close Father and I looked, with our dark hair and intense gazes.

I'd like to think they're both in Heaven watching us. Proud of what we've accomplished. Proud that we never once let ourselves be swept up in the glamour so intensely that we lost who we were.

"I love you," Elyse says, smiling softly.

"I love you more."

"I mean it, Isla. Thank you for thinking of me. I was worried you'd forgotten about me down there."

"Never." I could never forget about my baby sister. It's not in my blood. "You're the most important person in my life, Elyse. I will do anything for you, no matter what it takes. No matter how much it costs me."

She looks away, and I can tell she's fighting tears. "I wish I wasn't such a crybaby."

"It's okay to cry," I assure her, rubbing her back in small circles. There's no shame in crying. God knows

I did enough of that my first night here in Highburn. I can't remember a time in the beginning that I didn't end my nights by sobbing into my pillows.

"Okay, enough of the tears," she says, standing up and wiping her eyes. "I'm starving. Do we have anything to eat here?"

"Let's go down and ask the cooks if they have anything ready."

"Race you to the dining room," Elyse says. Before I can respond, she takes off running.

"God, you're such a brat," I groan. But she's my brat. She's here with me and Lowen, all of us together again. That's what makes it worth it in the end. That's the ending I would want were this a story my mother would tell me.

A happily ever after.

THE END

ACKNOWLEDGMENTS

Gonna be honest here, I'm not quite sure what this book was. A one-off exploration into the weirdest parts of my mind? The product of the pandemic? A stir-crazy creation that I probably won't ever try again?

Whatever it is, it's finished, and without a few people in particular, I never would've gotten the chance to write, "THE END." Without my lovely editor Kai's help, this would be some mangled block of text with dropped words and countless discrepancies, so I have to thank her first and foremost.

Next, I'd like to thank Katee Robert for writing so freely and joyfully that I was inspired to do the same. A retelling of *Beauty and the Beast* where the beast isn't some handsome white guy with a scar on his face and a bad attitude is a tough sell, but I wanted to write that book, so I did. Without Katee's tweets, ones where she lived her best life and wrote whatever the hell she wanted, I would've left this one in the drafts. No joke.

Then there's my writing group. Tasha L. Harrison is one of my favorite friends, and she and the rest of the Wordmakers writing community (hey, y'all!) motivated me to stop doom-scrolling through Twitter all day and actually put pen to paper. I also want to thank K. Sterling and Lucy Eden for doing our own little writing sprints together!

Of course, I have to shout out *Dr.* Katrina Jackson, HBIC, for always encouraging my ratchet ideas and essentially telling me, "this is the weirdest shit ever, Jack," and, "go write it. Now."

Last but not least, there's all my Twitter friends that I can't mention by name or else this thing will be just as long as the novella itself. You all stuck by me as I talked about this weird ass idea and even weirder sexual dynamic between Isla and Lowen, so you guys deserve your roses too.

Not sponsored, but I should also thank Express-VPN, because the amount of times I had to change my location to search things like, "what does a lion penis look like," or, "etymology of the word pussy" is kind of ridiculous.

No, the word wasn't used to describe genitalia until recently, and no, I don't care that I used it in this book. It is what it is.

ABOUT THE AUTHOR

Jack Harbon is your typical, eccentric twenty-something writing stories much more interesting than his real life. If he's not writing, he's either reading domestic thrillers about women in peril, watching trashy reality TV shows, or playing *The Sims*.

ALSO BY JACK HARBON

Encounters

The Babysitter (#1)

The Brother (#2)

The Intern (#3)

Sweet Rose

Meet Cute Club (#1)

Endearments

Daddy (#1)

Kitten (#2)

Standalones

Unwrap Me

Made in the USA
Coppell, TX
20 September 2021

62718692R00120